THE OTHER ME

"Peter," I said tentatively, once everyone else had left the room.

"Yes," he replied coldly.

I smiled. "Peter, I *really* do appreciate the fact that you take your job so seriously—"

He interrupted me. "Well, I wish you'd try taking *your* job more seriously," he snapped. Then he bolted out of the room and left me standing there alone.

Fighting tears, I walked back to my room to try to sort things out.

"The heck with him," I muttered angrily. "He didn't even give me a chance! He owes me *that* much, at least. Peter may be good-looking, but if he won't even listen, I'm not going to waste my time on him."

Bantam Sweet Dreams Romances
Ask your bookseller for the books you have missed

The Other Me

Terri Fields

BANTAM BOOKS
TORONTO · NEW YORK · LONDON · SYDNEY · AUCKLAND

RL 6, IL age 11 and up

THE OTHER ME
A Bantam Book / January 1987

Sweet Dreams and its associated logo are registered trademarks of Bantam Books, Inc. Registered in U.S. Patent and Trademark Office and elsewhere.

Cover photo by Pat Hill.

ISBN 0-553-26196-7

Published simultaneously in the United States and Canada

Bantam Books are published by Bantam Books, Inc. Its trademark, consisting of the words ''Bantam Books'' and the portrayal of a rooster, is Registered in U.S. Patent and Trademark Office and in other countries. Marca Registrada. Bantam Books, Inc., 666 Fifth Avenue, New York, New York 10103.

PRINTED IN THE UNITED STATES OF AMERICA

O   0 9 8 7 6 5 4 3 2 1

To Jeffrey, because I love you

Chapter One

"But he's *your* old college roommate," I protested. "Why do *I* have to miss a school dance just to see him?"

My father put his hand on my shoulder. "Paul Scherring and I have known each other for years, Jill. And he hasn't seen you since you were little. Can't I show off my lovely grown-up daughter?" he asked. There was a note of pride in my father's voice.

"Okay," I said, smiling. "The dance isn't that important, anyway. There'll be others."

As I spoke, I tried to picture my father as a college student. To me he'd always been just a father, and I couldn't imagine him walking around on a campus, doing homework, and dating girls that weren't my mother.

He hugged me. "Thanks, honey. I appreciate your changing your plans for me. We'll try not to bore you with *too* many reminiscences." He chuckled as he left the room.

I was still a little disappointed about missing the dance when Paul Scherring arrived the following night. He came in the door and I took his coat, but my thoughts were far away. I was wondering whether my best friend Angie would get up the nerve to ask David Masterson to dance with her that night. She'd been talking about it all week, and I was dying of curiosity.

A few minutes later, as I followed my parents into the dining room, I noticed that Mr. Scherring was going a little bald and he had a pot belly. *I gave up a night with my friends for him?* I thought. But when we got to the table, he held my chair away and pushed it under me as I sat down. I softened a little. At least he was treating me like an adult. I smiled up at him as he walked around the table to take his own seat.

He and my father began exchanging stories about their college days, and I found my mind wandering to one of my favorite daydreams: I was sitting on a balcony at night, under a star-filled sky with the sound of music floating out from a ballroom. A tall boy with sandy blond hair walked over to me, gazing at me from the depths of his clear blue eyes. He reached toward me and . . .

"Jill, what do you think?" Mr. Scherring asked, leaning across the table.

"I'm sorry," I admitted, feeling flustered. "I guess I wasn't listening."

"I was just telling your parents that I'd love it if the three of you could come to my resort this summer. I've always thought Scherring's Rose of the Rockies was the finest hotel in all of Colorado, but I think you should decide that for yourselves. I've been asking your dad for the past several years."

"From what you and my dad have told me, it sounds wonderful," I said.

"Don't get Jill's hopes up," my father interrupted. "I've got an engineering contract that's going to keep me tied up through the end of September. Summer is always my busiest season."

"And since Jim isn't going to be around much this summer," my mother added, "I've decided to go back to school for June and July and earn some credits toward my master's degree."

"You'll be the prettiest student on campus," Mr. Scherring said. "One of the smartest, too, I'll bet."

My mother blushed. I hadn't seen her do that since the time my dad had teased her because our paper boy had a crush on her.

"And what are your plans for the summer?" Mr. Scherring asked, turning to look at me.

"I'm not really sure," I said. He sounded genuinely interested. "I'll be sixteen soon, and I'd love to get a job this summer. But then, so would everyone else in my school. If this summer is anything like last summer, most of us won't be able to find work."

"That may not be so bad. A job can be very demanding," Mr. Scherring remarked. "It's a big responsibility."

I'd heard the same argument from my parents a million times. They didn't think I was ready to take on the commitment of a job. But I knew they were wrong. "Oh, I know it can be hard work, but that doesn't bother me. All I want is a chance. And I really believe that if someone gives you a job, you owe the company your very best effort," I said.

"Really?" asked Mr. Scherring.

I nodded, suddenly embarrassed that I'd gotten so carried away. *Jill, you idiot*, I scolded myself silently. *You sound like the world's biggest goody-goody.* Even so, I'd meant what I'd said. I just hadn't meant to say it that way.

"Are you sure?" Mr. Scherring asked, rubbing his chin.

"Yes. If someone's willing to take a chance on you by hiring you, then you have to prove that you deserve that trust."

Mr. Scherring was looking at me intently. "I couldn't agree with you more. Too many people do just enough to get by. They watch the clock without really putting forth any effort." He paused for a moment, looking from me to my parents and back again. "I'll tell you what. I don't usually hire sixteen-year-olds, but if you really want a job this summer, and you'd like to work at my resort, I think I can find something for you."

My mouth fell open, and I barely managed to say, "Do you mean it?"

"I sure do," he replied with a smile.

"Oh, that's very sweet of you, Paul," my mom began, "but you really—"

"What would the job be like?" I asked, interrupting my mother.

"Well, I have a professional crew for the whole year, but during the summer I hire a number of students to help the year-round staff. Everyone does a little of just about everything that needs to be done. They clean rooms, set tables, wash dishes. Some help run the stables—it's a pretty big resort, so nothing would get done if everyone didn't pitch in."

I could feel my cheeks begin to flush as I thought about the possibility of spending the summer in Estes Park, Colorado, instead of boring old California. It sounded so exciting— and if I was lucky, romantic, too. And I'd even get paid. Maybe I'd make enough money to buy some new fall clothes without having to look at every price tag.

"I think I'd love it," I exclaimed. But as I spoke, I could see my mother giving my father a worried look.

Mr. Scherring caught it, too. "Nothing has to be decided right now. Why don't we all just think it over for a while?"

By the time Mr. Scherring left on Sunday night, I'd quizzed him on every imaginable detail about his hotel. He had told my parents to let him know of their decision about my working at Scherring's Rose of the Rockies by the end of the month. That way he'd still have all of May to find someone else if I couldn't go. I could tell that my father was leaning toward letting me go, but my mother wasn't so sure. I figured I'd just have to wait and see.

At school I told everyone at our lunch table about Mr. Scherring's offer. My possible job at his resort came up again a few days later at one of Angie's slumber parties.

"Your folks have just got to let you go!" Pamela declared. "How could anyone turn down such an incredible opportunity?"

Angie scrunched her pillow up under her head and added, "I'd really miss you all summer, but I know you'd do a great job."

"I'd miss all you guys, too!" I assured them. The five of us—Angie, Pamela, Lori, Amy, and I—did something together almost every single weekend. "Remember last summer when we were going to make and sell those sand sculptures?"

"Do I ever! I thought for a while that my hand was going to become a permanent part of one," Amy replied.

"If I do get to take this job, I'm going to miss out on all the fun stuff here," I said.

"We'll write you every gory detail. And believe me, *all* of us would trade places with you in a second," Pamela said.

"Just think," Lori said, "Mr. Scherring will see what a good job you're doing there this summer, and then next year he'll be willing to hire us, too."

"I promise that if I can take this job, I'll do everything possible to get us all there next summer," I told them.

"That would be great," Amy added. "It would be neat if we got to do something that terrific. I get really sick of the Cyndi Norwoods of the world always having all the fun. And I'll bet even Cyndi's jealous of you!"

I had to smile at Amy's comment. The day before, in history class, Cyndi had come up to me as if we were best friends.

"I know how scared you must be, Jill—going away from home for the first time," she had said. "So you just tell that man who runs the hotel that he has to hire me to keep you company."

"You?" I had asked.

"Sure. If I come along, you won't be lonely at all," Cyndi explained. Then she walked away, leaving me standing by the classroom door. Cyndi could say things like that and get away with it.

I'd known Cyndi since the third grade, even before she had changed the spelling of her name—it was "Cindy" back then—to make it more unique. Since my last name is Novick and hers is Norwood, I'd been stuck sitting behind her in almost every class I'd ever been in. And because we're both about the same height and have long, brown hair, our appearances confused many teachers at first. But after we were in the same class for a few days, they'd never mix us up again. Cyndi was born bubbling charm and enthusiasm. And people—especially boys—usually fell for her act. I am quieter, more inclined to watch people and blend in, rather than wanting to be the center of attention.

When I first met Cyndi, I had wanted to be her friend. She was so talkative and friendly— all the things I'd wanted to be. But by fourth grade, she had apparently decided that I wasn't popular enough. So I couldn't help thinking that her sudden show of friendship in history class, after all those years, was peculiar.

"Cyndi *is* jealous," I said, telling my friends about the incident. "She actually said she wanted to come along to keep me from being lonely. Can you believe it?" Everyone laughed at Cyndi's "generosity." I didn't tell them that the sincerity in Cyndi's voice when she'd spoken to me had made me forget for a moment how phony she was. I mean, she *was* fun to be around. And I envied her poise. If she wanted to, Cyndi could make a new kid feel at home in ten seconds flat.

The next couple of weeks passed slowly. I did everything I could at home to show my parents how truly responsible I was—even cleaning my room and making my bed every single day. And those were two major accomplishments for me.

Scherring's Rose of the Rockies, I thought to myself one night as I lay in bed trying to sleep. The hotel sounded so romantic. There would be cozy fires to sit by in the evenings, and sun-dappled mountain streams to take long walks beside. I pictured the boy I would fall in love with there coming for a visit and taking me to the junior prom. But then I had to remind myself that I didn't have permission to take the job yet!

Finally, during the last week in April, I was heading up to my room to do some homework when I heard my father say to my mother, "Hon, we've got to make a decision about Jill. I told Paul I'd let him know by May first." I stopped in my tracks to listen as my father continued. "He was very nice to offer her the job, and I know that ten times as many kids apply as he can possibly hire." He paused for a moment as if he were choosing his words very carefully. "Katherine, I know you're afraid that Jill's not ready to leave home yet, but I think it would be a good experience for her. We've got to let her grow up, you know."

I strained to hear my mom's reply, but her

voice was too soft. I went up to my room and tried to start my French homework. But after a few minutes I put my pencil down. The suspense was killing me, and I longed to know what they were saying.

Finally, after what seemed like an eternity, there was a knock at my door. "How's your homework coming?" my dad asked.

"It's almost done," I said with a shrug. "I've just got a few more verbs to conjugate, that's all." But in spite of my attempts to act casual, I was dying to ask him if he'd made any decision yet.

"Well, good. When you're finished, Mom and I would like to talk to you. We'll be down in the family room watching TV."

"We could talk now," I offered. "I can finish this later." But he had already shut the door and left. Opening my French book, I raced through the exercises. *Who cares if I get a couple of things wrong?* I asked myself as I flew through the exercises. *I'll double check them during lunch tomorrow.*

Slapping my books shut, I ran downstairs and into the family room. "Jill," my mother said, "we need to begin to make some decisions about this summer."

Begin, I thought to myself. *I've been ready for two weeks.*

11

"Are you really sure that you want to be so far away from home all summer long?" Mom asked with a worried look on her face.

"You'd be jumping into a full-time commitment," my father said.

"I'm sure the Burger Palace is taking a few applications this summer," my mother said. "You'd still earn some money, but you wouldn't have to go so far away."

"Later on, when you're older," my father commented, "you'll have to go to work. Are you sure you want to take on such a huge responsibility just yet?"

I was sure that they had decided not to let me go. My mother was shredding a piece of tissue into tiny pieces, which meant that she knew she was making me unhappy, but she was doing it for my own good.

"OK," I said, my stomach in a tight knot. "I get the message. Are you finished yet?"

"Well, we wanted to make sure you'd really thought it out," my father said, "because if you have weighed all the pros and cons carefully, and you still want to go, you have our permission."

I leaped out of my chair. "Really?" I yelled. "Oh, I love you both. You won't regret it, I promise!"

My father looked at my mother. He took

her hand and squeezed it. "Our daughter seems pretty determined to go away, Kath," he said to her in a teasing tone. "If she wants to leave that badly, things must be awfully rough around here." My mother smiled back at him weakly, and I went over to her and gave her a huge hug.

"You know it's not that I'm unhappy here," I said. "I just want to try something new."

"Just remember to give it your best," my father said. "I still think of Paul Scherring as a good friend of mine even though I rarely see him. But he's not going to go easy on you because of me and I wouldn't want him to be."

"You'd better get a letter off to him tonight," my mother said to me. "He probably needs an answer right away."

I left them and headed upstairs to write the letter to Mr. Scherring. But first I had to tell Angie the news. I dialed her number, and when she answered I yelled, "They said I could go!"

"I just knew they'd let you!" Angie cried. "Oh, I'll miss you, Jill, but I'm so happy for you."

"Angie, you're the best friend anyone could ever have," I said, suddenly feeling a pang of loneliness because we'd be so far apart for the summer. "I've got to write Mr. Scherring now, but I'll talk to you tomorrow, OK?" She agreed and hung up. I started my letter, trying to keep it short, while still conveying the excitement I felt. I wrote several different versions before I came up with one that sounded right. I was afraid I was going to run out of stationery before it was perfect, but finally, I was satisfied with my efforts.

As I dropped the letter into the mailbox on my way to school the next day, I thought to myself, *Oh, Jill, this is only the beginning.*

A chill went down my spine. I just knew there was going to be something very special about the summer.

"Well, I did it," I told Angie when I met her at her locker in school. "The letter is in the mail. I just hope Mr. Scherring didn't give the job to someone else while my parents stalled."

"Don't be silly," she reassured me. "He's your father's old college friend. He isn't going to give your job away. Wow!" she said, her face suddenly lighting up with enthusiasm. "Wait until everyone finds out that you're actually going." Then Angie sighed. "I guess I'll try to get a job at Burger Palace. Of course, half the kids at school will, too."

I didn't say anything because I knew that

Angie was probably right. She sounded so forlorn that I made up my mind right then to write her lots of letters and find her a really nice present from Estes Park. "But just think, maybe next summer we'll all be there together," I added hopefully.

The bell rang, and as I walked to my first class, I tried to imagine what Scherring's Rose of the Rockies would look like. My mind conjured up visions of snow-capped mountains rising above a huge, elegant hotel. I hoped Mr. Scherring would write back soon assuring me that everything was settled. After all, until I heard from him, there was still the possibility that I wouldn't get to work at his resort.

I checked the mail every day, and finally a week later a big brown envelope from Scherring's Rose of the Rockies came for me. I could feel my heart pounding with excitement as I opened it.

The first thing that fell out of the package was a scrawled note to my parents from Mr. Scherring, saying that he was glad they had decided to let me come and not to worry about me. I pulled out a letter addressed to me. "Welcome aboard, Jill," it read. "I'm delighted to have you as part of our team. Let me know your travel plans, and I'll arrange to meet you. Please plan to arrive by June seventeenth. Best, Paul Scherring." Enclosed was a form letter with the details of my room and board. It said I'd be rooming with one of the other girls who had been hired. I'd earn one hundred and fifty dollars a week and be able to buy all my meals for under five dollars a day. There was also a color brochure of the resort showing tall pine trees surrounding the sparkling white hotel with purple mountains in the background. There was also a photograph of one of the hotel rooms, which was large and luxurious. It was one of the fanciest bedrooms I'd ever seen. For a moment I wondered what my room would be like. But I didn't really care—it was exciting enough just to be going there.

Later that night my parents and I looked over the brochure together. "Well," my dad said, teasing me, "now that we've seen the brochure, I guess we should toss it out. Or did you want to keep it for something?"

I grabbed it. "Don't you dare! I'm going to take it to school tomorrow and show everyone. Then it's going up on my bulletin board, so I can see it every night before I go to sleep." My mother laughed along with my father and me. After she'd read Mr. Scherring's note, she seemed much more relaxed about my decision to go to Estes Park.

The next day at lunch, I pulled out the brochure to show Angie and the others. But before they could see it, obnoxious Don Anderson grabbed it out of my hand.

"Let's see what Jill is so excited about," he teased. He stared at the brochure for a minute. "Wow, check this out." He began reading from the brochure: " 'Join us for an early morning ride on some of the Rocky Mountains' most beautiful trails. Sit by the olympic-sized pool and sun yourself, or join our exercise instructor for a morning workout. Dine on your private balcony or eat in our elegant dining room. Jacques Rouquille, our award-winning chef, will make certain that your every meal is prepared to perfection.' " Don stopped reading and looked at me. "Why would such a classy place want to hire someone like you?"

Some of the kids thought that was hilarious. "I'm almost sure I hear a little jealousy," I said, taking the brochure from him. Mr. Scherring had said that he didn't usually hire people my age. I hoped that that meant I would be around mature boys instead of jerks like Don.

"You know," said a girl at the end of the table, "you are really lucky. I'd give anything to be able to work at such a gorgeous place."

"I just wish the summer would hurry up and get here," I replied with a smile. "I can't wait."

Chapter Two

That weekend, however, I realized that there would be a scary side to going to Colorado for the summer. My parents and I were having brunch at my Aunt Anne's apartment, and toward the end of the meal my aunt turned to me. "Jill, honey, you must be bored to death. Why don't you go down to the pool. My neighbor's daughter is home from college, and she's invited some of her friends over today. I told her about you, and she said you were welcome to join them."

Aunt Anne was right: I was bored. But the thought of meeting a lot of strange, older kids scared me. The adults were watching me expectantly, so I excused myself. After changing into my bathing suit, I headed down to the pool.

Stepping through the sliding glass door that led to the pool, I walked across the white tiles. Three guys and two girls were laughing and talking, and I could feel butterflies in my stomach. I usually stuck to my own group of friends at school, and it had been a long time since I'd had to try to fit in with a new group. As I got closer to them, I noticed how handsome the guys were. They looked like the kind of boys Cyndi Norwood could snuggle right up to—the kind of boys I was afraid to even talk to. But they'd already seen me, so I knew I couldn't turn back. I took a deep breath. "Hi, I'm Jill, Anne Hullman's niece," I said in a friendly voice.

"Oh, she said you might drop by. Pull up a chair," said an elegantly poised girl with long red hair. "I'm Sally, and here are Louise, Mark, Brendan, and Jamie."

"Nice to meet you," I said, trying to sound casual. But as I pulled a lounge chair closer, it screeched across the cement and stopped their conversation. "Sorry," I said, "I guess I should have picked it up." I sat down on the chair, and it collapsed.

The boy named Brendan jumped up. "Are you OK?" he asked. He picked up the broken chair and set it on a stack of others by the side of the pool house. In my embarrassment, I stuttered, "F-f-fine, I'm really fine."

"Well," he said, as he brought me a new chair, "you certainly know how to make an entrance."

I was too mortified to say anything. I couldn't even force myself to smile. Instead, I sat there silently, and after a while I think the other kids forgot I was there.

An hour later, I got up quietly and walked back to Aunt Anne's apartment. *What had ever made me think that I could talk and flirt with a whole new group of kids—especially when they were so much older than me?* It wasn't just that the chair had collapsed—it was the whole way I'd handled it. If I had only made a joke about it, everything would have been fine. Suddenly, I realized that there was a major flaw in my summer plans—me.

I wasn't going to be with my own little group in the summer. I was going to be left all by myself. It would be awful to be the only one without any friends, the only one who didn't go to any parties. But maybe it wasn't too late. Even though I was aware of the consequences, I decided right then to tell Mr. Scherring and my parents that I didn't want the job. My dad would be angry, Mr. Scherring would never offer me another job, and my mom would say that she'd known all along that I was too young to handle such a big responsibility. But I didn't care.

Leaning against the wall in the hallway of Aunt Anne's building, I thought about my decision. It was one thing to have to tell my parents, but what could I say at school? Practically everyone knew that I'd gotten the job— even the really popular kids. They would think that I had either lied about having gotten the job or that I was a total fool for turning it down. But even more important than what the other kids thought of me was what I thought of myself. Could I live with myself knowing that I had run away from my first big chance to do something exciting with my life?

Oh, why hadn't I thought of how impossible it would be for me to fit in with the resort staff *before* I'd gotten myself into this mess? I knew I'd always been tongue-tied around strangers, but somehow I'd been so caught up in getting the job that I'd just forgotten about it.

I was very quiet on the ride home. My mom asked me once if I was OK, but there wasn't any way I could explain my feelings to her. If I backed out, I knew she'd be very understanding. But every time I wanted to prove my independence later on she'd say, "Remember when you thought you wanted to work at that resort?" I'd be defeated from the start.

When we got home, I went to my room, shut the door, and stared in the mirror. The hazel-eyed reflection wasn't bad. My long brown hair was thick and had just the right amount of curl. I knew I could stand to lose a couple of pounds, but no one would ever look at me and think I was fat. In fact, there wasn't that much difference between my looks and Cyndi Norwood's. She certainly wasn't any prettier than I.

But I had a feeling that there was another reason why guys fell all over themselves for Cyndi. She might not always be sincere, but she was up on whatever was the latest and a lot of fun to be around. She knew all the right things to say to make anyone feel as if she were her best friend. But I could tell from watching her that Cyndi's best friend was Cyndi herself. Still, as phony as she was, the boys seemed to adore her. But it didn't impress me. In fact, one night when Angie had slept over, I'd imitated Cyndi's fake friendliness for her.

"You've got her to a tee," Angie had cried,

choking back her laughter. "It's almost spooky. I feel as if she's right here in this room."

"Remember when she hadn't studied for her history test, and she tried to get poor Joel Silverman to help her?" I had asked. Angie shook her head.

"Oh, Joel," I'd cooed, in Cyndi's whispery voice. "If I were only as smart as you are, I wouldn't have to worry about this dumb history test." I pouted the way Cyndi had.

Angie had joined in, dropping to her knees in front of me. "Please don't worry, Cyndi," she pleaded, lowering her voice to sound like Joel, "I'll help you get through this test, one way or another."

"Of course," I'd said to Angie in a flat tone, "Cyndi had her way and poor Joel ended up giving her almost *all* the answers."

Angie had gotten up from the floor and was still laughing.

Then I had stood up and walked over to my mirror. Cocking my head to one side, I studied my reflection. In Cyndi's sulkiest voice, I said, "I'm sorry, girls, I just can't go along for a pizza today. You know how it is." I pulled one of my pockets inside out to show that it was empty.

Angie had waved her hand around wildly

and said, "That's OK, Cyndi, it's our treat. *We* invited *you*."

"So Cyndi Norwood gets to have pizza, and the girls get Cyndi's company," I had remarked, turning back to face Angie.

"She's so phony," Angie had said.

"I know. But girls really are glad to have Cyndi along with them because the boys come over to their table to see Cyndi. And even if there are no boys around, Cyndi makes lots of jokes and keeps the conversation going."

"Don't defend her, Jill," Angie had said. "I don't trust Cyndi—and I sure don't trust the people who put up with her nonsense."

Then we'd stopped discussing Cyndi, and I didn't really think much about that night later. But thinking about it then made me realize that if Cyndi had gotten my job instead of me, she wouldn't care that she was only a sophomore and all the other kids were seniors or college kids. She could walk into a roomful of strangers, and leave having made friends with the most popular kids there.

I flopped down on my bed in disgust. For an instant I pictured myself stomping up to Cyndi and screaming, "You can have my job. You've got the right personality for it." Then I'd turn and leave. Boring old Jill Novick would have a nice, boring summer at home. It would work, too—Cyndi could go and pretend to be me. The only person she'd have to worry about running into would be Mr. Scherring. I smiled, thinking that even if I were boring in California, I'd be popular in Colorado.

Then I remembered what Angie had said: "*I feel as if she's right here in this room.*"

Sitting up, I got an idea. If I could send Cyndi with my name, why couldn't I send myself with Cyndi's personality? I shook my head. I couldn't. It was too risky. But then, my best friend thought I had imitated Cyndi perfectly. Of course, Angie didn't know just how far I'd go.

I began to pace the length of my room. "Think of the pros and cons," I said out loud. The advantages were obvious. Cyndi would be outgoing, she'd never be at a loss for what to say, she'd be able to put other people at ease, and she'd have a great time. The only disadvantage was a big one: *Could I actually pull it off?*

I still had a few weeks of school left. Instead of just casually observing Cyndi, I could really study her. Of course, it would have helped if we were friends and I could have seen her in every situation, but we weren't. Still, I did see her in four of my classes, and I could watch her from a distance at the last school dance. I might just be able to do it. It was worth a try.

The next day I bought a new red loose-leaf notebook so I could write down everything I learned about Cyndi. I'd keep track of her every gesture, her every response. Then I'd go home and study them.

By the beginning of June I had the notebook filled with "Cyndi-isms." I practiced being Cyndi in front of my mirror, trying out her affectations until they sounded natural. It seemed to get easier, too—at least in the privacy of my room. And at school, when I listened to people talk to her, I began to be able to predict what Cyndi was going to say and how she would say it.

For instance, one day in French class, I saw Allan pass by Cyndi's desk. I knew she was going to comment on his letter sweater. Half a minute later Cyndi said, "Neat, you've got your track letter sewn on your sweater already. It looks great." Then at lunchtime I saw Rick sit down at Cyndi's table. I was pretty sure she was going to say something about his well-known love of chocolate. As I listened in, I heard Cyndi say, "Since I know how much you like it, Ricky, I'm going to let you have my piece of devil's food cake." It was hard to conceal my delight from Angie and the others at my table.

By the time school got out, I was sure that I could manage to act like Cyndi while I was at Scherring's. Her mannerisms and breezy speech would never be easy for me, but if I was careful to think before I did or said anything, I could do it. I also decided to change my name—I'd call myself Jillian. It had a sophisticated ring to it, and I was sure that Cyndi herself would have approved.

No one would know about my plan, not even Angie. She disliked Cyndi even more than I did. She'd probably think that the whole idea was dumb and try to talk me out of it. Angie was the greatest friend in the whole world, but when it came to being around guys, she was less sure of herself than I was. She didn't worry about it, though. She said she was prepared to wait for some guy to come along who liked her despite her shyness. But I wasn't willing to wait. I wanted to go away, have a great summer, and prove to myself and everyone else that I wasn't just boring, shy old Jill.

I walked home after my last class and

flopped down on the living room couch to read what kids had written in my yearbook. We tried to get as many signatures as possible every year. Sometimes I ended up asking kids whom I'd barely spoken to all year to sign my yearbook.

As I leafed through the glossy pages, I noticed one message in particular. It was written in lavender ink and read: "Good luck this summer. I only wish it were me! Have a great time!" It was signed simply: "Cyndi."

"Well, Cyndi," I said smiling to myself. "In a way, you *are* going to Estes Park this summer."

I threw away most of my folders and notebooks from school, but I tucked the red "Cyndi" notebook away in the bottom drawer of my desk. I made a mental note to remember to pack it. Suddenly it occurred to me that I didn't have any Cyndi-type clothes. Fortunately, there wasn't much that I really needed to buy since all the employees got a uniform when they arrived at the resort. I'd sent Mr. Scherring a note telling him when I'd be arriving and I'd also given him a list of my sizes. His secretary wrote back to say that my uniforms would be waiting for me when I got there.

*   *   *

Angie and I went shopping the day after school was out. As I walked out the door, my dad called after me in a teasing tone, "Don't spend all your money before you've even earned it."

Angie and I went to the mall near my house. When we arrived at a large department store, we headed straight for the junior department. "Oh, look," Angie said. "Here's a cute top."

She was holding up a pink blouse with light blue flowers on it. I loved it, but it didn't look like something Cyndi would have picked out. Reluctantly, I left it on the rack.

"Didn't you like it?" Angie asked, puzzled.

"It was all right," I said, shrugging. "But let's keep looking."

By the time we'd finished shopping, I had a headache. Angie and I hadn't agreed on a single thing I'd bought. "I guess you're a little nervous, huh?" she'd said at one point.

I nodded. "I'm getting on a plane on Monday that will take me hundreds of miles from home, and I'm going to spend a summer working at a job I know nothing about, with a bunch of people I've never met. How would you feel?"

"Petrified," Angie admitted. "But you've always been braver than I."

*   *   *

Angie came over to give me a going-away gift on Sunday. It was stationery decorated with mountains. I don't know if it was the gift or the thought of saying good-bye to Angie, but I just couldn't talk. She hugged me. "You're going to be fine. Don't worry! I'll sure miss you this summer." Her eyes were filled with tears, and I could feel mine filling up, too. I hugged her good-bye and promised to write faithfully. Then she left.

By the time I finally finished packing that night, it was almost ten o'clock. I decided to go to bed early, but I was much too nervous to sleep. My mom came in a little while later and sat on the edge of my bed. "I'm sure going to miss you, honey," she said.

"Gee, Mom, it isn't going to be for *that* long. And you and Dad can always come visit me," I said. I was trying to be really brave so I wouldn't break down and admit how terrified I was. "Besides, the stereo won't be blaring, and the phone won't be tied up for the whole summer!"

Mom laughed and hugged me. Then my dad came in. "We're so proud of you," he said. "I know you're going to be the best employee that Paul Scherring has ever had." Then they kissed me good night, and left. I felt so homesick—and I hadn't even left home yet!

                        *   *   *

It's going to be worth it, I told myself the
next morning as we headed to the airport.
*It's going to be the best time of my whole
life.* I looked down at my suitcase. I was holding it so tightly that my knuckles were white.
Despite my calm appearance, I was scared
and shaking inside. Just thinking about
boarding an airplane alone for the very first
time made me cringe with fear.

Numbly, I checked my baggage and walked
toward the gate. A few minutes later my flight
was called, and I hugged my parents good-bye.
I never looked back even once as I walked down
the ramp to the plane. I knew that if I turned
around to wave I'd probably start crying. As I
entered the plane, I handed the flight attendant
my ticket, and she directed me to my seat.

By the time the plane had started down the
runway, no one had taken the seat next to
me. I buckled my seat belt and listened carefully to the flight attendant as she instructed
us on what to do in case of an emergency.
Then the pilot's voice came over the speaker.
He sounded calm, and I relaxed a little. *Well,*
I thought as the plane began to speed down
the runway, *ready or not, Colorado here I
come.*

Chapter Three

As we got closer to Denver, I pulled out my instructions from the resort. I already knew them by heart, but I wanted to read everything over once more. I was to land at Denver's Stapleton International Airport and take a bus from there to Estes Park. Once I was at the Estes Park depot, I'd be met by a resort staff member. It all seemed clear enough. I just hoped that my baggage wouldn't be lost and that I'd be able to find the bus stop at the airport without any trouble.

We landed, and as soon as I got off the plane, I headed for the baggage claim area. All the luggage was just beginning to slide down the carousel, one bag at a time. I kept waiting for my bags to come through the little chute, but there wasn't any sign of them. My nervousness was coming back, and just as I was about to go to the lost and found, my smallest bag slid down the ramp. My bags and luggage carrier were the last three items to come into view. With a sigh of relief, I loaded my suitcases onto my luggage carrier and began to look for the bus stop to Estes Park.

I had to ask for directions from three different people, but I finally found the right spot. There was only a sign, though, indicating that it was a bus stop. *Where am I supposed to get my bus ticket?* I wondered. An older woman who was standing at the stop told me that her travel agent had sent it to her with the airline ticket. I waited for the bus for fifteen agonizing minutes, hoping that the driver would let me get on. Then, figuring that I could always pay at the bus station in Estes Park, I tried to calm down. The bus finally pulled up. I looked at the driver as he opened the door; his face looked grim. I didn't think I'd get any sympathy from *him*. After waiting for the driver to load everyone's luggage on, I stepped up and said, "Uh, excuse me, but I don't have a bus ticket yet. I really need to get to Estes Park, but I promise I'll pay for it as soon as I get there. And I'd be glad to show you that I do have the money."

The bus driver pushed his hat back on his head. "Don't you worry, young lady," he assured me. "I'll be back as soon as the bus is loaded up, and then you'll get your ticket."

"Oh, OK," I said. Two guys were laughing at me. I made my way to a seat feeling as if I'd aged a decade from just worrying, and I hadn't even gotten to the resort yet. When the other people had boarded the bus, the driver walked down the aisle, collecting fares. I smiled weakly as I paid mine.

"A lot of people get confused about how to pay," he said. "Don't worry about it."

As the bus wound its way out of the crowded Denver area toward the mountains, I finally began to relax again. The scenery was beautiful, and I knew my parents would love it. Then I thought how stupid I was. *Cyndi* would not have been thinking about her parents. Suddenly I began to wonder if I was really going to be able to act like Cyndi. I could do it in a familiar setting like school, but if the rest of the summer was going to be like today, I was going to be too confused and worried to be someone else. I would have enough trouble just being *me*. And if no one liked plain old Jill Novick, then I would just have to endure a lonely summer.

The bus pulled under the awning attached to a small building marked ESTES PARK BUS STOP. Opening the doors, the driver got out, and I followed him. As I stepped off the bus, I noticed a lanky boy in a white T-shirt and faded jeans waiting nearby. Although I knew it was rude, I stared at him. He was gorgeous! He looked rugged with sun-streaked blond hair and tanned arms, but there was a twinkle in his blue eyes. He was watching me, too. *If I ever have a boyfriend,* I thought, *I want him to look like that.*

The driver handed me my luggage, and my daydreams of boyfriends ended as I gathered all my belongings together. The muscular boy I'd admired took a picture out of his pocket, looked at me for a minute, and then walked over to me. "Hi," he said, "I'm Peter Wilson, and I'm here from the Rose of the Rockies to pick you up. Mr. Scherring asked me to send his apologies. He wanted to greet you himself, but he got tied up at the last minute. I hope you won't be upset with the substitution."

Upset? I thought. *This is wonderful!* His voice was deep and brisk. In a split second three things went through my mind. First, I wanted this boy to like me. Second, there was no way plain old tongue-tied Jill would ever get noticed by a guy as handsome as Peter. Third, Cyndi Norwood would know exactly how to get him interested.

"Well, hello!" I said in a voice that sounded way too flirtatious to really be me. "I'm Jillian, but then I guess you know that. I think I've just discovered one more terrific thing about this place. Are *you* on the staff?" I cocked my head and looked up at him just the way I'd seen Cyndi do many times. My decision on the bus to just be myself that summer was irrevocably changed. For better or worse, I'd just begun the ultimate deception.

Peter nodded as he picked up my bags and carried them over to a waiting Jeep. "What a cute car!" I exclaimed, remembering that Cyndi always told boys she liked their cars.

"Yeah, it's fun to drive. I like driving a stick shift, and I love the openness. You really feel like you're out in nature." Peter climbed into the driver's seat, and I sat on the passenger side. "Have you ever been to Estes Park before?" he asked.

"No, I've never even been to Colorado before," I replied.

"Well, everyone will be glad to show you around. You're going to love it."

"Oh, I'm sure I am," I murmured. It was too noisy to talk after he started the Jeep. I breathed in the clean mountain air and gazed at my surroundings. The ride to the resort wasn't too long.

"Well, here we are," Peter called out over the engine. The pride in his voice was obvious. The resort was set into a mountain, and it appeared gleamingly white beneath the blue sky. The trees around it were lush; the fresh pine smell was almost overwhelming. "Leave your bags here for now," Peter said. "I want you to see the place as a guest sees it for the first time. Then I'll show you to your room."

We walked into the lobby. Huge picture windows looked over the trees, and I could see a sparkling lake in the valley below. The lobby's ceiling must have been twenty feet high; the room was decorated in the blues, greens, and yellows of the outdoors. I stood there in amazement, forgetting for a moment all about Cyndi and Peter—forgetting everything except that I was going to spend the summer in this perfectly beautiful place.

Peter continued to show me around. The swimming pool was huge, and it had a fountain in the middle that shot up into the sky. Around it were flower beds that overflowed with color. There were a Jacuzzi, a sauna, and a steam room, as well as an exercise room where an instructor was leading an aerobics class. We walked out into the garden.

I felt intimidated. "The grounds are so big. I hope I don't lose my way around."

"Don't worry. There will be lots of people to help you. And each room has a map, just in case you do lose your way."

We arrived at the tennis courts next. Peter said, "They are covered with the best playing surface available—it plays like clay but it dries in less than an hour—and all of them are lighted for night play." He pointed off toward a shady mountain slope. "Most of the nature walks begin over there. Charley, the guy who leads them, was born and raised around here. He knows the name of every rock, tree, bug, and flower in the area."

"Do employees ever get to take his hikes?" I asked, thinking how wonderful it would be to walk along the trails.

Peter looked amused. "It could probably be arranged." He took me back inside and showed me the dining room, which was done in soft peach shades that reminded me of a sunset. Then we climbed up a magnificent white staircase to the second floor.

The guest rooms were enormous. "How many people do they expect to stay in one room?" I gasped. My bedroom back home would have fit in one tiny corner; the room was almost as large as Aunt Anne's whole apartment.

Peter laughed. "I take it that you're impressed."

"Impressed?" I blurted out. "I'm scared to death. This place is perfect. Maybe I should have waited a few years to work here. I don't want to ruin anybody's vacation." Then I blushed and wished I could take back every word I'd just said. Cyndi would never have done anything so dumb. I'd just been so overwhelmed that I'd forgotten to think like Cyndi.

"Don't be embarrassed," Peter said in a reassuring tone. "You should see the reaction of most of the guests when they open the doors to their rooms for the very first time."

Peter's eyes sparkled, and he changed the subject. "Mr. Scherring says your family knows him well, so you must know that he's an absolute marketing genius. There's not another resort in Colorado, or maybe even in the whole country, that begins to compare to the Rose of the Rockies. He found the perfect spot for the resort, and he was smart enough to realize that many people want to be part of nature for a little while. But they also want luxury—and that's just what he gives them.

I'm planning to major in hotel management when I start college this fall, but I know I'll learn more from Mr. Scherring than I will in all four years of college."

"You already know so much about the place," I noted.

"Well, that's because I've been coming here with my parents every year since I was eight. By the time I was thirteen, I was already begging Mr. Scherring to give me a job. He promised that if I'd wait until I was fifteen, he'd give me a chance. I was the youngest employee here when I started. I remember that first summer, and how scared I was." He winked at me. "It all worked out pretty well, though, and I'm sure you'll be happy here, too," he said.

"Oh, I hope so," I said. "I mean I'm really going to try to do my best." I almost winced after I'd said that. It sounded like a Brownie Scout pledge.

Peter seemed not to have noticed. "Actually, we're both pretty lucky. You can't imagine how many kids apply for jobs here every summer."

Peter ended our tour at the staff's quarters. The area reminded me of my cousin Alice's college dormitory.

"You know," he remarked, "not everyone

41

who works at the resort lives here. You get less money and work more hours if you do, but you have a lot more fun.

"Well, this is the girls' hallway, and this is where I leave you. Your suitcases should be waiting for you in room three. Get yourself settled." He glanced at his watch. "It's one o'clock now, and you're supposed to report to your first staff meeting at four-thirty. I'll see you then. And Jillian—don't be scared. It's going to be an outstanding summer."

Peter waved and left. As I watched him walk down the hallway, I thought he was absolutely the most handsome, wonderful boy I'd ever met. If I could just be around him, it really *would* be an outstanding summer. Mesmerized, I stood in the hallway long after he'd disappeared from view.

Shaking my head, I walked to room three and opened the door, wondering if my roommate would be there. She wasn't, but it looked as if she'd made herself right at home. As I looked around, I noticed she'd taken the larger of the two closets, the bed by the window, and three of the five dresser drawers. Suddenly, I just needed to sit down and sort things out.

My thoughts were running in a thousand directions at once. There I was, hundreds of miles from home, on the verge of a summer I knew was going to be special. The resort was even more beautiful than I had dreamed it would be, and Peter—he was a boy right out of my most romantic daydream. *Maybe he'll even like me*, I thought. But I had my doubts. He probably had his pick of the girls at Scherring's. Why would he want me? All I'd done since I'd arrived was look and act like a scared child.

But Peter *had* been very nice to me. Then I cringed. Maybe I reminded him of himself when he was younger, and he just felt sorry for me! I was mortified. After all my hard work, I'd failed miserably at being Cyndi. So far, anyway. Maybe it wasn't too late. From then on, I'd have to bury *me* so thoroughly that even if I were scared, or tired, or mad, the real Jill wouldn't pop through. If I just worked hard enough being Cyndi I would get the most wonderful boy in the world to notice me. I hugged myself. "OK, Cyndi," I said out loud, "First things first. Just how are you going to handle this little roommate situation?"

I knew how *I* would handle it—I'd say nothing. Or maybe I'd confront her right away and tell her that she wasn't being fair. That would get us off to a bad start. Either way, I'd lose.

What would Cyndi do? Just then, my roommate opened the door. She seemed surprised to see me, even a little annoyed. She was dressed casually in shorts and a navy-blue cotton knit shirt, but there was something very sophisticated about her. Her hair was blond and sleek. The way she leaned against the door told me that she was very confident.

"Oh, I forgot you were coming today," she said. "I'm Lisa. I guess we're going to be roommates this summer."

Think, Cyndi, I told myself, putting on my brightest smile. "I'm Jillian," I said. I walked to Lisa's open closet door. Cyndi would make her aware of the difference in closet size without actually saying anything. "That's a nice shirt," I said, turning back to face her. "You're so lucky to be able to wear navy. It looks so pretty with your blond hair. I just look like a dark blob whenever I wear navy-blue." I lingered at her closet just a minute too long— the way Cyndi would have—then I walked over to my own closet and opened the door. Anyone would have noticed that mine was smaller, but I didn't mention it. I hung up my jacket while Lisa watched. Then I opened the top drawer of the dresser. "Ooops," I said, "sorry, I didn't realize that it was yours." I counted down and opened the third drawer. "Oh, gosh, I guess this is yours, too." I looked up and smiled at her.

"We could split that third drawer if you want," Lisa said quickly.

"That's OK." I shrugged nonchalantly and said nothing more. I leaned over to unlock one of my bags, then looked up at the window by Lisa's bed. "What an absolutely fantastic view!" I exclaimed. "I feel so lucky to be here. This summer is going to be the best, and I know we're going to get along together." I cast my eyes down at the bed, feeling like an actress in a play. "I just want this summer to be perfect in every way. You know what I mean?" I asked.

Lisa knew just what I meant. She smiled at me, and I sensed that we were going to be friends.

"I think we should change one little thing," she said. "It really would be fairer if you got the bed by the window."

"Oh, Lisa, you don't have to do that. I mean the view is great. Why shouldn't you get to wake up to it?" I asked, trying to sound innocent.

"Because I've already got the big closet and

one more dresser drawer. I insist that you take the better bed," she said.

"Well, if that's really what you want," I replied, shrugging. As we transferred her bedding, I tried hard to contain my amazement at how well I'd maneuvered things. It could only get easier from here on. I'd be Cyndi in every way, and the world—and Peter—would be at my feet.

"You know, I was really depressed when I first found out we were rooming together," Lisa said, watching me as I unpacked. "I thought it would be such a drag to have the youngest staffer for a roommate."

The old Jill would have apologized for forcing herself on someone like Lisa. But not Jillian. "I may be young," I said, "but I don't act it." I looked Lisa right in the eyes.

"Oh, I know," she said. "I can tell. We're going to get along just fine."

I went back to my unpacking. Lisa was silent for a few minutes, and then she stood up. "I'll come back for you before the staff meeting," she told me. "They're kind of dull, but at least you can meet some of the kids then."

"Thanks," I replied. "See you later." Lisa left me alone, and I stopped unpacking and sat down on my bed, staring out the window.

I could do it. I could have the summer of my life by using every Cyndi trick in the book. I dug through my open suitcase and pulled out the worn red notebook. I wouldn't need it, but I was glad I'd brought it along. Because that notebook contained all my secrets for making this summer my best ever. And it was only just beginning.

Chapter Four

As Lisa and I walked toward the meeting room later that day, I kept looking for Peter. I wanted to thank him for the tour, and I also wanted to make a better impression on him. *If only I'd concentrated more on the way I was supposed to act when I'd first arrived, Peter would be the one looking for me. Well,* I thought as we reached the doorway, *maybe I'll get a chance to start over with Peter now.* Three or four people were in the room when Lisa and I walked in, but Peter was not one of them. I didn't want to depend on Lisa, so I walked toward a girl who was sitting in the corner.

"Don't bother with her," Lisa whispered. She guided me toward a small clique that was gathering outside the door, and introduced me to everyone.

I saw her exchange an approving look with a girl named Traci. Lisa nodded her head, as if she were answering a question. Traci turned to me. "You'll really love it here. The gang has a lot of fun together." Her dark ponytail bobbed as she spoke, and her big brown eyes glowed.

"Look who's talking like an old pro," one boy said. I liked his impish grin. He turned toward me. "Traci's been here for five whole days, so she thinks she knows everything."

Traci stuck her tongue out at him. "Big deal, Andy, you've only been here a week."

Normally I would have been content just to listen to their silly insults, but I knew that Cyndi would have imposed her presence on everyone. "Well, I'm sure glad to finally be here. Where's everyone from?" I asked.

In a few minutes I was the center of attention, and I felt as if I'd been there for weeks.

"So, tell me," Andy said, "what are you going to be doing around here?"

I realized that I had no idea what my job was going to be. I'd been so busy convincing my parents to let me come here that I'd never bothered to find out exactly what I'd be doing. Then I told myself to calm down. Cyndi wouldn't care what her job was. With a smile and a careless laugh I hadn't tried out until just then, I said, "From what I've heard so far, I may get assigned full-time duty just trying to keep you out of trouble."

"Score one point for Jillian." Traci laughed.

At that moment Peter walked into the room. I caught his eye, and he started to smile. He looked carefully at the people I was standing with. *Good,* I thought, *he knows I'm not the same wimpy kid he showed around earlier.*

"Well," he said, "I see you've all met Jillian. She is the most recent and final addition to our summer staff. Now, if everyone will please take a seat, I'll get this meeting over with quickly."

I sat down, wondering why Peter was conducting the meeting. Did everyone have to take a turn? I hoped that my turn would be a long time coming if that were true. It seemed more likely that Peter was in charge; he *had* been the one to show me around. The room got quiet, and Peter started talking. "I know many of you need to be on duty soon, so I'll make it brief." I looked around the room and counted ten people.

"Is this the whole staff?" I whispered to Lisa.

"No way," she whispered back. Peter glared at us, and I suddenly felt as if I were back in school.

"I think everyone except Jillian has their permanent job assignments now," Peter said. "We tried to honor your requests, while taking into account your previous job experience. If you get bored or want to try something else, we'll try to arrange a switch. But it's up to you to observe and learn about the new job for at least three days before requesting a switch. We'll vary shifts, too, so those of you who have evenings off now will get days off later, and vice versa."

Peter continued through his list of announcements, moving so quickly from topic to topic that I was getting confused. But everyone else was following along, and since Peter kept referring to a "packet," I figured that I'd catch on as soon as I had all my materials. Soon the meeting ended, and people hastily left the room.

"Jillian, can you stay for a minute?" Peter called out. I could hardly believe my good luck. I'd spent the last few minutes trying to figure out a way to approach Peter, and now I was going to have my chance.

"Mr. Scherring wanted you to stop by his office for a couple of minutes," he said.

"How nice," I said, gushing. "Are you going in that direction?"

Peter gave me a peculiar look and said, "Yes, as a matter of fact I am." We began walking. "You certainly seem to have made friends fast."

"Well," I said with a wink, "I started out with a great guide to show me around." I took a breath. "You know, I really liked the way you ran the meeting. You handled everything so well."

"There really wasn't much to it," he replied, looking slightly annoyed. I began to wonder if something was bugging him. "There's Mr. Scherring's office," he said. Peter turned to leave, but before he did he looked back at me. "Oh, by the way, Jillian, why does he just call you Jill?"

Feeling rebuffed, I didn't answer, walked toward Mr. Scherring's office, and knocked on the open door. "Jill," he said warmly. "Welcome! I'm so glad you'll be with us this summer. Well, what do you think so far?"

I told him in glowing terms just how I felt about his resort. "It's absolutely beautiful. After seeing this place, I don't understand why anyone would want to go anywhere else in the whole world," I told him.

Mr. Scherring chuckled. "I may have to let you write our next brochure. I knew I'd done a wise thing when I hired you. You just keep up that enthusiasm, and I know you'll be one of our best staffers."

I cleared my throat. "Uh, Mr. Scherring, exactly what am I going to be doing here?" I asked.

"Let's see." He pulled a chart out of his drawer. "Well, based on what you told me while I was visiting your family, your only work experience has been baby-sitting. So, we've made you the assistant children's activities director," he said.

"Oh." I wasn't sure exactly what that was, and I didn't want to say the wrong thing.

Mr. Scherring said, "The director of children's activities, Margaret Francis, is a kindergarten teacher, and she'll help you with any problems. Of course, before the summer is over, you'll get a chance to try your hand at some other things, too, but the assistant children's activities director is a very important job. If the children aren't happy, the parents will book their next vacation someplace else," he finished.

Then with a flourish, he handed me a big blue spiral notebook and three uniforms. "You'll read all about when to wear them in the manual," he said. "And, Jill, don't be nervous about this summer. If I didn't think you could handle the job here, I wouldn't have hired you—no matter who you were. As a friend of your father's I'm always here if you need me, but as your employer, I won't give you any special treatment. Actually, we'll have very little direct contact—you'll be answering to Peter Wilson for the summer. I think you'll like him. He's very fair, but he demands that everyone do a good job. He's young, too, but I've got no qualms about putting him in charge of all our summer employees. He's a most outstanding young man," he said, almost to himself.

I thought, *Don't I know it. The only problem is how to make him think I'm a most outstanding girl.*

Mr. Scherring seemed distracted, so I excused myself. I was back in my room by six, planning to spend the evening going through the employee materials he had given me. Lisa wasn't there, so I sat on the bed and opened the manual. "Employees at Scherring's Rose of the Rockies are far more than just employees. They are the very heart of what makes this resort run." I was jarred from my reading by the ringing of the phone.

"Hello," I said uncertainly.

"Jillian, this is the switchboard. Peter asked that you report to the lower rec room as soon as possible."

I put on my shoes and tried to remember how to get to the lower rec room. Then, just as I was going out of the door, the phone rang again. "Is this Jillian?" asked a male voice.

"Yes," I replied, "I'll be there right away."

"Now that's what I like," the boy said. "I haven't even asked, and you've already accepted."

"Who is this?"

"Oh, now that hurts. I can't believe you said you'd go before you even knew who it was," he said.

By that time, I'd figured out that it was Andy. "Several of the kids are going into town to see a movie," he explained. "Will you come with me?"

"Duty calls," I said forlornly, just as Cyndi might have. "It's an emergency, and I'm the only one who can handle it."

"Poor thing," Andy said. "Is that what they told you?"

I glanced at my watch and realized I'd been talking to Andy too long. "Listen, I've really got to go," I said and added, "but I want to get together soon." I hung up the phone and dashed downstairs toward the rec room. I was excited about seeing Peter, but I was worried that I'd kept him waiting. When I got there, Peter was going in the other direction.

"Did you just get here?" he asked as we passed each other.

I was still pleased with the way I'd handled Andy, so I said in a joking tone, "Hey, it wasn't an easy choice to make. This wasn't the only offer I had tonight, but I'm here."

"Then get to work," he said coldly and continued on his way. I knew I wasn't *that* late. But before I could figure out what had gone wrong, I walked into the rec room and promptly forgot about Peter.

There must have been about twenty kids of various ages there, and all of them were running around. One harried woman was strumming a guitar and trying to keep their attention. When she saw me, she put down the guitar with a sigh of relief.

"Am I ever glad to see you," she said. "I'm Margaret Francis."

"Hi, I'm Jillian," I replied.

"We can talk later. As you can see, we've got our hands full right now. There were only supposed to be five children down here tonight—the rest were last-minute drop-offs, and I don't have enough different activities for all of them. Do you want the older kids or the younger ones?"

I stood there with my mouth open. I had no idea what to do with either group. "Tell you what," she said, "I'm beat. Would you mind if I take the little ones and read and sing to them? You can take the older kids outside and organize some games that will use up some of their energy."

Automatically, I hustled all the seven-, eight-, nine-, and ten-year-olds outside. I could think of only two things. First, I didn't know what to do with them, and second, I was freezing. The mountain air was cold later in the day.

"Well, what are we going to do out here?" asked a dark-haired little girl. "I'm bored."

The thing I'd learned about kids from baby-sitting was that they usually saw through lies, so I replied, "I'm not sure. You look pretty smart. What do you think we should do?"

"Build a fort," she said.

"Yeah," agreed another kid.

"Great idea!" chimed in an older boy.

I asked the first little girl how she wanted to build the fort.

"We can cut down the trees and put them together," she replied.

The other kids cheered at the suggestion, but I quickly convinced them that we could gather twigs and rocks instead. Everyone was assigned a partner. "No one leaves this area," I said. "Now—go!" The kids scattered in all directions and soon returned with the first load of materials. They had a little trouble keeping the walls from collapsing when first they started building it, but things went pretty well after that. The kids seemed to enjoy what they were doing, especially after the girls and boys split up, each group trying to build a better fort than the other. The time passed quickly, and when parents started arriving to pick up their kids, I was surprised and a bit disappointed that the evening was over.

After the last child had left, I walked back into the rec room. I was completely frozen. Margaret had already put away the indoor toys because the younger children had left by eight. "You were great out there, but you look awfully cold. Want to get a cup of coffee?" she asked.

I didn't usually drink coffee, but at that point anything hot sounded good. We wound our way up to the employee cafeteria, and when the smell of food hit me, I remembered that I hadn't eaten anything since my early lunch on the plane. I ordered a hot ham sandwich, a bowl of soup, and splurged on a huge mug of hot chocolate. I sat down next to Margaret, who was sipping her coffee.

"Well," Margaret said, "I'd hoped to get you into all of this a little more gently, but Peter noticed how swamped I was tonight. He said he was sure you wouldn't mind coming down to help. I hope tonight was a fluke, but maybe we're just going to have lots more kids around this summer than we did last year."

Margaret explained that parents could sign their children up to stay with us from one in the afternoon until nine at night, and it was our responsibility to have something available for the kids to do. "It's my third summer working here, and I really love it. I'm a teacher, so you'd think I'd stay away from kids during the summer. But I've had other summer jobs, and this one is perfect for me," she said. I liked her a lot, and I could tell that she liked me. I wasn't going to have to worry about putting on Cyndi's personality around her, or the kids.

"Well," Margaret finally said, "I'm tired, and I'm sure my husband is waiting for me to get home. Why don't we meet here about noon tomorrow and go over all the toys and supplies then? We have seven kids signed up for tomorrow afternoon, but people add and cancel right up to the last minute." She pulled on her sweater. Since I'd finished my dinner, she showed me the window where the employees stacked their dirty dishes. Then she left.

*   *   *

When I got back to the room, Lisa still wasn't back. I wondered if she'd gone to the movie with Andy and the others. It felt good to know that they'd liked me enough to think of inviting me, and it was especially exciting because I had a feeling that they were the *in* group at the resort. I smiled, realizing that I might actually have the chance to be one of the popular ones.

As I got ready for bed, I thought about my own long day. I was so tired that I was practically asleep on my feet. As I got into bed, I thought again about Peter. He had seemed so cool and distant at the meeting and then down by the rec room. *Well,* I thought, *I shouldn't let that upset me. I was late getting downstairs to help Margaret, so of course he'd be a little annoyed with me.* I rolled over and fluffed up the pillow under my head. Peter would see what a hard worker I was. And, with any luck, he'd notice that I wasn't a bad friend, either. After all, the summer was just beginning. And *Jillian* had just arrived.

Chapter Five

The next morning, I glanced at the little digital clock on my night stand, sure that it was about six o'clock. It seemed as though I'd just fallen asleep. I could hardly believe it when I saw that it was past ten! Sitting up with a start, I looked at Lisa's bed. She wasn't there. I'd slept so soundly that I'd never even heard her come in the night before or get up in the morning. I stretched and wondered if I'd ever get a chance to get to know her. Of course, acting like Cyndi would be easier if I didn't have to be around any one person for long, at least until I'd had more practice.

I saw the staff book on my dresser, and my heart started pounding. *Oh my gosh*, I thought, *what if Lisa's at some kind of staff meeting that I was supposed to be at, too?* I could imagine Peter glaring at me, but this time it wasn't my fault. I had planned to read the staff book after the meeting, but I'd had to work. I picked up the book and opened it. Some loose sheets of paper in the back described the role of the assistant children's activity director. I skimmed through them quickly. They said my work hours were from one to nine PM, so at least I wasn't supposed to be on the job yet. Figuring I'd read them later, I tucked them away. I leafed through the rest of the book and found a section on staff meetings. They were held once a week, at three different times during the day. That meant that no matter what shift I worked, I'd be free to attend one meeting. The book went on to say that sometimes meetings were called for more than once a week. But as far as I knew, I wasn't missing work and I wasn't missing a meeting.

I opened the window next to my bed. A soft cool breeze carried in a tangy pine scent. I saw a group of people on horseback riding down a mountain trail in the distance. Flopping back down on my bed, I took a deep breath. *I'm really here!*

My stomach growled. I didn't know what time lunch started, but I was sure it was still too early. I'd have time to read the manual, find out about the resort, and grab a bite before I met Margaret.

I opened the book and, to my surprise, found out that I'd have to take a test about Scherring's Rose of the Rockies next week. According to the manual, "Every employee is a public relations agent for this resort. You need to know and appreciate all the things that make it special, so that no matter what a guest asks you, you can answer with pride." Peter would probably give the test. I made up my mind right then and there to show him that I'd learned all this stuff perfectly.

I read for over an hour. My stomach growled fiercely, so I flipped to the section on meals. "Employees have the option of purchasing inexpensive hot meals or making selections from snack machines in the employee cafeteria." Anything sounded good.

Since I was meeting Margaret at noon, I wasn't sure if I'd have time to change clothes after lunch, so I decided to wear my uniform. *Well*, I thought to myself, *here goes nothing. I hope it fits.* I had seen everyone else wearing these uniforms, and actually, they were quite flattering. I slipped on a bright yellow polo shirt, the kind that all Scherring employees wore. The female employees wore blue split skirts, and male employees wore blue pants. I pulled on the skirt and zipped it up. I stood on my tiptoes to see myself in the little mirror Lisa had propped up on the dresser, and I decided I didn't look bad at all. Better yet, the outfit was comfortable. The bright yellow shirt gave my brown hair a rich, reddish shine. I put on some lipstick and started out the door, wondering if I'd see Peter at lunch. I went back and dabbed on a little of my favorite cologne. Then I headed down to the cafeteria.

I guess I'd been expecting to see Andy or Lisa or one of the kids I'd met the night before there. But looking around, I didn't see a single familiar face. Even though I was hungry, I felt like beating a hasty retreat back to my room. I didn't want to eat alone. If Peter came in, he'd think I was a reject. As I stood in the doorway, I forced myself to imagine how Cyndi would handle the situation. Then I walked over to a table. "Hi, guys, I'm Jillian, the new kid on the block. I'll trade you a piece of chocolate cake for a place at your table."

"I love chocolate cake," a boy said, laughing, "and I like your style." He moved over to make a spot for me on the bench. Within minutes, I had finished my lunch, the boy—

Greg—had eaten my cake, and I was in the middle of a conversation with a group of kids. Fifteen minutes later some members of the group were already scurrying back to their jobs, but several of them told me to be in the same place at the same time tomorrow. It was just that simple. I was in. The Cyndis and Jillians of the world had it easy.

It was just about noon, so I cleared my place and went to find Margaret. She was just setting up some things. "I'm glad you're here," she said. "It will give me a chance to show you some of the equipment we have available for the kids." I was intrigued by an enormous lightweight ball—as big as a small child—that was used in group games. There were also lots of different building sets, paints, clay, puzzles, and games. "We also have the option of taking the kids to the pool. And once a week, usually on Mondays, the wranglers will take any child over six, who wants to go out, for an afternoon horseback ride," Margaret said.

I laughed. "It sounds pretty good to me. I wouldn't mind being a kid here myself. I'll bet they love it."

"It's up to us to make sure they do. From the way you handled those kids last night,

I'm sure you're going to be a big asset in making that happen," she remarked.

I blushed. Margaret was really a nice person. She'd be easy to work with.

"Well," she said, "the kids will be arriving soon. We don't have too many signed up this afternoon, so I think we'll just let them play for a while, and if they start getting restless, we'll plan something more structured."

"What do the parents do while the kids are here?" I asked.

"Oh, some get in a round of golf, some play tennis, and some just want an afternoon of peace and quiet. Mr. Scherring tries to make sure that parents have as much family togetherness as they want, but that the kids can be kept busy when their parents want a break."

From the corner of my eye, I saw Peter coming through the doorway. As he walked over to us, I flashed a smile at him. He didn't even acknowledge my presence.

"Margaret, are you all set for today?" he asked.

"Sure, Jillian's going to be a great help," she told him.

Peter looked at me quizzically, as if he didn't quite know what he thought of me yet. Then he said, "I see that you've got your uniform."

This was my chance. With my hands on my hips, I shook my head slightly so that my hair would swing. "Yes, I did. Do you think it looks OK?" I asked him.

Peter's blue eyes seemed to pierce right through me. "Maybe you should try that on someone else," he said. He turned and began walking out of the room. Margaret was looking through a book and didn't notice his abrupt departure.

I couldn't believe it. Was Peter jealous? Of whom? The only boy he'd ever seen me with was Andy. I had to set that straight immediately. It would be so stupid for Peter to stay away all summer just because he was jealous. I boldly followed Peter out of the room. "Wait up a sec," I called. He stopped in the hallway. When I caught up with him, I tilted my head and gave him my most inviting smile. "You never answered my question," I said, smiling. "And it's really *your* opinion I want."

Peter looked at me reproachfully. "I think these uniforms are crisp and neat-looking. They're also easy to take care of. Beyond that, I don't really care." His tone was cold. What had I done wrong? Before I could come up with an answer, Peter said, "I'm sure Margaret is waiting for you." He turned on his heel and left.

I was stung by his dismissal. I walked back to the rec room and looked over all the supplies. The time passed quickly, and soon kids began to arrive. I noticed a little girl sobbing into her blanket. My heart went out to her. Margaret had her hands full with a group of kids, so I sat down on the floor to talk to the girl. The name tag pinned to her shirt said "Nancy."

"Hi, Nancy. My name is Jillian," I told her. She looked up at the mention of her name, then buried her head in her blanket again.

I wondered if she was frightened or upset about being left here, in strange surroundings, without her mom and dad. If that was it, maybe I could get her involved in something that would distract her from her fear.

"I'll read you a story," I offered. But Nancy just shook her head and clutched her blanket. I came up with several other suggestions, but nothing seemed to work. Finally I walked over to Margaret and whispered, "I don't know how to get that little girl to stop crying. Do you know why she's so upset?"

"I'll come over there as soon as I get these kids started playing dodge ball. She didn't want her parents to leave her. Stay with her until I get there. OK?" I returned to Nancy's side again. As I sat down, I noticed that there was a big duck embroidered on her blanket.

"Wow," I said. "I wonder if your duck is friends with my duck? Let me show you my duck, and we'll see." The little girl took her head from her blanket. I pointed to the duck I'd found when I'd gone through the stuffed animals with Margaret, and then I solemnly introduced the two ducks to each other. "I'm glad you came to play," my duck said. Nancy giggled and held her duck closer to mine. "I'm glad *you* came to play," I told Nancy, in my normal voice. She smiled. For the rest of the afternoon, she played quietly, never letting either her blanket or the stuffed duck out of her sight.

Margaret took most of the kids to the pool for about an hour and let them work off some of their energy. There were only a few kids left by dinnertime, so we took them to a large table reserved for us in the dining room. The formal beauty of the dining room seemed to put them on their best behavior, so the meal was peaceful.

At eight o'clock, after the last child had been picked up, Margaret told me I could leave an hour early. "Oh, I don't think I should do that," I said doubtfully. "Are you sure there isn't anything I can do here?"

Margaret waved me out of the rec room. "Don't feel guilty. You'll more than make up the time on the days when parents show up an hour late," she said.

When I got back to the room, I expected it to be empty. I was surprised to find Lisa flopped on her bed, reading a book. "Hi, stranger," she said, putting it down.

Although I was exhausted, I managed to drag Cyndi out.

"Stranger, named Jillian Novick, reporting in for debriefing," I quipped. Lisa laughed, and the two of us sat down to find out more about each other.

"I'm on kid patrol," I told her. "What's your job?"

"I requested waitressing. I figured if I ran short of money at school next year, I could always apply for a job in a nice restaurant and put this place down as a reference. Then I found out I'd been assigned to duty as a bus girl because I had to get experience with food service before they'd let me waitress," Lisa began. "I work breakfast and lunch and help set up for dinner. Then I'm off, so at least I've got my evenings free. Of course, I have to be dressed and in the dining room by seven A.M. so if I stay out too late, I can't tell the difference between a fork and a spoon. But I've definitely got my priorities in order," she said, pausing. "Who really needs to know the difference between a fork and spoon anyway?"

I laughed, and Lisa asked me how I got my job assignment. "Well, jobs at home are so tight that the only experience I had was baby-sitting, so I was made the assistant children's activities director. Believe me, that's just a fancy name for baby-sitting." I wanted to sound as detached from my job as she was, so I didn't mention that I liked Margaret or that the kids were sweet. "The two great things about my job are that I can sleep late in the morning and I still get off work early enough in the evening to party," I said lightly. I looked at Lisa to see what she thought. I didn't want to sound too wild.

"Well," said Lisa, leaning toward me a little, "that's what I like to hear. So, who do you have your eye on—or do you already have a boyfriend? You got here a little late, so I'll fill you in on who's available and who's not."

I wanted to ask her about Peter, but I didn't know Lisa that well. I knew that Cyndi wouldn't reveal anything confidential about herself until she had most of the facts.

For all I knew, Lisa could be Peter's girl-friend!

73

I shrugged, and avoided a direct answer. "I don't have a boyfriend, and I haven't really had a chance to meet very many people here yet. Just the group that you introduced me to last night before the staff meeting, a few people I sat with at lunch today, and Peter," I said. *Say something about Peter,* I urged silently.

Lisa wanted to talk about someone else. "I like a guy named Bill Harding. You haven't met him yet, and when you do, stay away," she said. Her tone was teasing, but I had the feeling that she wasn't joking.

The two of us sat up talking until well past midnight. I was tired, and I was afraid that I wouldn't be able to keep up my Cyndi act much longer. It was hard to weigh every word and still make sure my conversation sounded natural. All my practice in front of the mirror seemed to have paid off, though. I didn't slip even once.

When we turned out the lights, Lisa said in a sleepy voice, "You know, if you need some extra space, I'll split that third drawer with you. And you'll have to meet the rest of the group. There's a party in the grove tomorrow night. Why don't you come right after you get off work?"

Lisa rolled over then. Soon I could hear her

smooth, even breathing, and I knew she was asleep. I was wide awake. With a pounding heart, I realized that not only would I be at the party with all the popular kids, but that I'd have a chance to see Peter again. I began to imagine our meeting. The night would be crisp and cool, and the only light would be the glow from a small bonfire. We'd back away from the rest of the crowd, into the trees. Peter would take me in his arms, and there, under the stars, we'd plan our summer—together.

Chapter Six

If working with the children the next day hadn't kept me on my toes all afternoon, I would have done nothing but worry about the party. But between coaxing three five-year-olds to share the paint supplies and helping Margaret keep track of a pair of mischievous twin boys, I was too busy. Finally the last child was gone, and I was free to leave.

I said good-bye to Margaret and walked toward the staff quarters. As I walked, I realized that I should have asked Lisa what she was wearing to the party. I might not see her until it was too late to change. She might have even forgotten that she'd invited me. But my biggest concern was that Cyndi's personality might desert me midway through the party. If I lost my bubbly charm, I'd be totally exposed.

While I was getting ready, I decided to curl my hair a little. It wouldn't last long, but at least I'd look good when I first walked into the party. I turned the ends under with a curling iron as I debated what to wear. I ignored the fact that Lisa hadn't left a note for me. What had she said anyway? Had she said she'd meet me somewhere other than our room? I pulled on a pair of white baggy jeans and a striped green shirt. What if she was standing somewhere waiting for me, and getting really angry? I had just decided to go out looking for her when she bounced through our door, looking flushed and happy.

"The party is great," she said. "I almost forgot that you didn't know where it was. Come on."

Lisa was wearing a sweatshirt that said "University of Colorado" and a pair of blue jeans. My jeans and shirt had turned out to be the right choice. We headed away from the resort, and I heard music playing faintly in the distance. A couple of minutes later, we came to a clearing in the trees. A bunch of kids were dancing, laughing, and just standing around talking. There was no campfire, but a portable generator provided electricity for some lights and the cassette player.

Lisa spotted Bill. "There he is," she said. "Some hunk, right?" I nodded. "Have fun, Jillian," Lisa added. "See you later." She ran over to Bill, leaving me all alone. My stomach felt as if it were flopping around, and I fought an urge to run back to my room. But if I did that now, I'd be out of everything for the entire summer. I'd never have a chance to get to know Peter.

Well, come on, I told myself sternly. *Don't let the party happen without you. Cyndi wouldn't.* I strode over to Andy. He was busy talking to some other people, but I knew him by name, and he *had* flirted with me a couple of days earlier.

"It looks like everything started without me," I said to Andy. My voice sounded lively, and no one would have guessed how scared I was.

"Don't worry," he said. "We save the best part for last."

"What's the best part?" a boy who was standing nearby asked. He had a deep voice and spoke slowly. He grinned lazily at me.

"The best part," I said, "is that Andy is just about to introduce me to you." The boy's grin grew wider.

"Jillian, you don't know what you're saying," Andy groaned. "Watch out for this guy."

"She can take care of herself," the boy said.

"Jillian, I'm Todd. Would you like to dance?" While everyone watched, Todd led me over to where the other couples were dancing.

After a few songs, we went back to the group. I saw Andy give me an appreciative look, and I realized that I was no longer scared. I laughed and chatted with everyone as though they were long-lost friends of mine. *This is what I've always wanted*, I thought. I was the center of attention, and I was popular. But deep down inside, I didn't feel as happy as I'd thought I would. I tried to convince myself that I was feeling disappointed because Peter wasn't there. But that was only partly true. Sure, I wanted a chance to convince Peter that I really wasn't as terrible as he obviously thought I was. But part of my disappointment was because of something else—something I couldn't quite put my finger on.

Andy grabbed my hand and interrupted my thoughts. "I love this song, let's dance," he called over the music. We danced together for the rest of the night, and by the time the party was over, my feet hurt so much that I could hardly stand up. Andy and Todd both walked me back to the staff quarters. We parted at the hallway leading to my room, and I was relieved because I could finally let my guard down.

Lisa wasn't in the room. *She's probably with Bill*, I thought.

As I drifted off to sleep, I thought how strange it was to be home from a party and not to have anyone know I was back. No one here cared what time I came in or where I went, as long as I showed up for work, ready to do a good job. Cyndi would have said that the independence was awesome. And I had to admit that I did feel very grown-up. But I felt a little lonely, too. My mom always waited up for me at home, and we'd sit in the kitchen together, drinking tea or hot chocolate and talking.

Well, I decided as sleep overtook me, *I have to grow up sometime.*

I slept soundly. I never even heard Lisa come in. The next morning I woke up feeling refreshed. I pulled open the drapes immediately, to let the sun in. "It's so bright," Lisa murmured.

"Lisa," I said with surprise, "I'm sorry, I thought you'd be at work already. What are you doing here?"

"That's all right," Lisa said stretching. "I wanted to get up and wash my hair anyway. And to answer your question, I'm off this morning."

I leaned back against my pillows. "Thanks for inviting me to the party last night. It was really super."

"Well, *I* thought so," she said, "but I may be biased. If Bill's there, I'm happy." I wanted to ask her why Peter hadn't been there, but I didn't. Cyndi always got her information in a more subtle way.

"The grove is really perfect for a party. How'd you find it?" I asked.

Lisa looked surprised. "I thought you'd know about it. It was set up as a picnic ground for the children's activities program." She laughed. "Of course, after the kids are safely tucked in their beds, it's a great place for the big kids to play. It's far enough away so that no one at the hotel can hear the music, and there's enough room for people to dance."

That was my opening. "Were most of the kids from the resort summer staff program there?" I asked.

"Are you kidding?" she replied. "Have you seen a lot of them? They aren't exactly our type, if you know what I mean."

"I guess you're right," I said, pretending to think about it. "I don't think I saw Peter there. He's not bad looking."

"Oh, you mean Peter Wilson," she said. "He's cute, but he kind of keeps to himself, I guess. Are you interested?"

I smiled. "It's always fun to meet someone new," I replied. That comment seemed to satisfy Lisa. She started talking about some of the other things the group had planned for the summer. From the way she spoke, it was clear that I would be invited to everything.

When Lisa went into the bathroom to wash her hair, I decided to write to Angie. Pulling out a sheet of the stationery she had given me, I found I had no trouble writing about the resort itself or about my job as the assistant children's activities director. "Don't be too impressed," I wrote. "The title sounds very official, but the job is a lot like babysitting, only instead of one or two kids, I've got up to about ten or twelve to keep track of."

"There are other benefits, too," I wrote. "The people I've met are really nice. I'm the youngest one here, but I've already been accepted as part of an older gang. At a party last night I danced with two guys—Andy and Todd." I couldn't tell Angie about my feelings for Peter Wilson. I wasn't sure I understood those feelings. We had only been together once, the day I arrived, and he hadn't shown any sign of interest. What was it about him that made my heart start to pound the moment I saw him?

I'd just finished the letter when Lisa came back into the room, her hair full and shiny.

"Well, that's done. Are you going to lunch?" she asked me.

I realized then that I'd missed breakfast again. "Yes—but I'll have to get into my uniform," I said.

A few minutes later, we were walking down to the employee cafeteria. "I think we're in for a dynamite meal today. Yesterday, the chef made a ton of crab salad because he expected it to be a big seller, but it didn't sell well at all. So today we'll pay a dollar fifty for the same meal they paid seven ninety-five for in the main dining room yesterday," Lisa said.

"Is that how it works?" I asked. "Well, I'm crazy about crab." Several people called out to us as we entered the cafeteria. I realized that I knew a lot of people there. It should have made me feel good, but since none of the people who called out were Peter, it wasn't as thrilling.

The conversation at our table was light-hearted and relaxed. I got so caught up in the playful banter that I was almost late for work.

"Hello, Margaret," I said, entering the rec room.

"Jillian, would you like to take the kids to the pool today?" she asked me. "It's only fair to split the fun stuff," she added, winking.

"But be sure to put on a sun block, or you'll burn."

"You'd better go, Margaret," I said. "My swimsuit is in my room and I probably shouldn't leave you to go and get it."

"Nonsense," Margaret said briskly. "If you hurry, I won't even know you're gone."

I didn't want to appear to be taking advantage of the situation, so I practically ran back toward the staff quarters. But as I turned a corner, I nearly bumped into Peter. My first impulse was to just keep going because Margaret was waiting for me. Then I stopped. This was an opportunity that Cyndi would make the most of. "Well hello, stranger," I said warmly.

"Aren't you supposed to be working now?" he asked me.

"That doesn't mean I can't be friendly, does it?" I said, giving him one of Cyndi's pouty looks. "Margaret sent me back to get a bathing suit," I added. "I'm taking the kids swimming." That sounded defensive, but I couldn't help it. "Really, it's true," I said. "I wouldn't just take off when I was supposed to be working. This is just the greatest job. The kids are darling, and Margaret is super." *Cool it, Jill,* I thought, *Cyndi wouldn't gush about her job.*

"Some of those kids can be quite a hand-ful. I've worked in recreation a few times my-self," Peter said. He fell into step with me, as friendly as he'd been the first day. I was so excited, I hardly heard a word he said. When we arrived at the girls' dorm wing, I knew I should hurry away to change my clothes. Mar-garet was waiting with all those children, and she'd been extra nice to let me have the after-noon at the pool. On the other hand, it was the first time I'd had a chance to talk to Peter. If I gave the conversation a few min-utes to warm up, maybe he'd ask to meet me later. I leaned against the wall, well aware of how Cyndi would handle the situation. "What did you say about working in recreation?" I asked, looking earnest. "Go ahead and tell me. I'm sure Margaret expects me to be a few minutes."

I caught a troubled look in Peter's clear blue eyes. "On second thought," I said, "why don't you wait right here? It'll only take me a minute to change clothes, and then, if you have time, you can walk me back to the rec center and finish telling me your story." Pe-ter didn't say anything, but I knew he was watching me walk down the hall toward my room.

I shut the door behind me, and then I

jumped up and down in elation. I was glad I'd splurged on a new black-and-white polka-dot bathing suit. I put it on, swept my hair up into a side ponytail—Cyndi wore her hair that way at the pool at home—and whisked on a little Summer Coral lipgloss. I reached for the baggy T-shirt I usually used as a cover-up, then stopped. My mom had given me one of her beach cover-ups, a short little robe made of gauzy white cotton. I put it on and tied the belt. Glancing in the mirror, I knew I looked great.

I wanted to make a real entrance. I wanted those big blue eyes of Peter's to widen when he saw me. Pasting a big smile on my face, I reached for the doorknob. I pulled open the door. "Peter," I said, savoring the name, "I'm ready." But there was no one there.

I was alone in the hallway. Peter was gone.

Chapter Seven

Two days later there was a notice on the bulletin board about an extra staff meeting. Peter had signed it. I was still angry with him for abandoning me in the hallway, so I felt like not showing up at the meeting. *But then you won't see Peter,* I told myself. It was true. He'd been rude, but it hadn't completely crushed my interest in him.

When I arrived in the meeting room, Peter was standing near the front with one of the guys who I knew worked in the stable. I couldn't hear what they were saying.

Peter looked gorgeous. He'd taken advantage of the fact that we didn't have to wear our uniforms to meetings and had on a pair of khaki pants with a light blue polo shirt that accented his eyes and made his hair seem lighter. I just couldn't be mad at him. He hadn't actually said he'd wait for me that day, and I knew Peter was a busy person. He'd probably had to take care of something important, and I couldn't have expected him to come knock on my door and tell me. Maybe, if I could get his attention, he'd apologize. I walked toward the front of the room, but as I got closer, I changed my mind. The stable hand looked very upset, and I didn't think I should interrupt their conversation.

Lisa had told me that a summer worker had accidentally let a horse escape, and it had taken four people almost an hour to corral it again. I had the feeling that this was the guy who'd done it. He looked very contrite. "Listen, Peter, it was a stupid thing to do," he said loudly. "I should have rechecked that south gate before I left. If you want to shift me out of the stable to something else, I wouldn't blame you."

"Tony, quit apologizing," Peter replied. "Anyone can make a mistake. The wrangler says you're one of the most thorough guys down there, and I know you'll be even more careful from now on. Give yourself a break and quit feeling so bad about it."

No wonder Mr. Scherring had put Peter in

charge. It would have been so easy to make the stable hand feel miserable, but Peter had gone out of his way to restore Tony's confidence in himself.

As soon as Tony had walked away, Peter asked everyone to take a seat. "I'll try to keep this short," he said. "I know that most of you would rather be doing something else—and I can't blame you!"

He covered some general information, then said, "As you know, the philosophy here is that whether the resort succeeds or fails depends on the employees. I'd like to read you a letter of which I'm very proud." He held up a note and began reading. " 'I travel quite often, and I'm usually too busy to write to the hotels where I've stayed. But I wanted to tell you that my visit at Rose of the Rockies was exceptional. The atmosphere was wonderful, and the food rivaled any I've ever enjoyed. One of the most important things I look for in a hotel is cleanliness, and, at Scherring's, my room was always immaculate. I'll be back again.' "

He put the letter down and looked at us. "We checked the computer records for the dates and the room where Mr. Stitter stayed. Two of our summer employees, Pat and Sandy, were the girls on maid service for that room.

I think we ought to give them a hand," Peter declared.

The two girls blushed, and Peter said, "It may not seem very glamorous or important to be dusting and making beds, but you can see what a difference it makes." He was beaming. I was sure he had the most beautiful smile I had ever seen.

Our eyes met. His smile disappeared. "On the other hand," he said, with a hard edge to his voice, "there are a few people here who feel it is quite appropriate to go to their work stations unprepared and then wander back to their rooms to get what they've left behind. They don't seem to care how much extra work they leave others to do."

The other employees in the room looked a little confused, but I knew exactly to whom he was speaking. I felt myself flush with anger. Peter was being completely unfair. I'd had no way of knowing that I was going to take the children swimming. I'd even offered to stay in and let Margaret take them! I was going to straighten things out right after the meeting.

I tuned out the rest of the meeting. I didn't mind being scolded if I had made a mistake, but I hadn't done anything wrong. I sat in my chair, fuming. Margaret said I was a natural with the kids, and a terrific help! Peter owed me an apology, and I would demand it!

Then I tried to figure out how Jillian should handle this. I couldn't remember Cyndi ever telling a boy off. She'd always charmed them into whatever she wanted done. Okay. I'd try it Cyndi's way. Her way had helped me since I'd arrived at the resort. Why change now?

"Peter," I said tentatively, once everyone else left the room.

"Yes," he said coldly.

I smiled. "Peter, I *really* do appreciate the fact that you take your job so seriously—"

He interrupted me. "Well, I wish you'd try taking *your* job a little *more* seriously," he snapped. He bolted out of the room and left me standing there alone.

Fighting tears, I walked back to my room to try to sort things out.

"The heck with him," I muttered angrily. "He didn't even give me a chance! He owes me *that* much, at least. Peter may be good-looking, but if he won't even listen, I'm not going to waste my time on him." Cyndi Norwood had never chased a boy, and neither would I. With new resolve, I put on my uniform and ran down to the rec room. I took a long, circuitous route to avoid running into Peter. I'd already decided to skip lunch because I'd had a huge breakfast before the meeting.

Margaret was rounding everyone up. She greeted me and said, "I was going to take the kids fishing today, unless you mind." Just the thought of putting a worm on a hook made me a little queasy. Even though I loved working with the kids, I was sure that I wouldn't be able to make myself do it. In fact, the only thing I could think of that would make the situation worse would be to have to take the fish off the hook.

"Uh, Margaret—maybe I should stay back here with the kids who don't want to fish," I suggested.

"They all seem to want to go," Margaret said. "And I think we'll have our hands full."

We all walked to a nearby lake with our fishing gear. A little boy named Bobby who had bright red hair, freckles, and two missing teeth stayed close to me. "Do you like to fish?" he asked.

"Well," I said, hedging, "it's going to be fun today. Have you ever been fishing before?"

"Yep," he said matter-of-factly. "My dad's been taking me to the lake ever since I was little."

I smiled. "Where are you from, Bobby?"

"We're from Denver. We come every year," he said.

We arrived at the lake. Margaret took six children, leaving me with four, including Bobby. They looked expectantly at me. It was time to help them bait their hooks. I opened the container of worms, but after one look at the squirming mass, I closed it again.

"Let's spread ourselves out a little bit," I said, trying to smile. "Then I'll give each one of you a fishing rod, and help you put it in the water."

The children did as they were told, and the first one I approached was Bobby. I handed him a fishing pole. "We'll be all set in just a minute," I told him.

His big brown eyes looked at me skeptically. "Jillian," he said, "can I ask you something?"

"Sure," I said, grateful for anything that would postpone the baiting of his hook.

"Are you scared of worms?" he asked.

I looked at Bobby and began to grin. "Yes, I guess I am. Silly, isn't it?"

"No. I used to be scared of monsters at night. Want me to bait the other kids' hooks?"

"Bobby," I said, "I'd really love that." He could tell I meant it with all my heart.

In a few minutes Bobby had baited everyone's hook. Each child was watching the water. They all looked so hopeful. I wanted Bobby to catch one, but I didn't want to have to take the fish off his hook.

I sat down on a rock behind the children so that I could keep an eye on all of them. The sun beat down on my back, and the leaves rustled in the gentle breeze. The children were talking among themselves. My bad mood from the run-in with Peter had faded, replaced by a wave of contented well-being.

We'd been fishing for about an hour without any luck when Margaret signaled to me to start packing up. Bobby had just begun reeling in his line when he screamed, "I got one! I got one!" The other children threw down their rods and ran toward him. Sure enough, he had a small fish flopping around on the end of his line.

"It's just a baby fish," Bobby said. "I'm going to throw it back."

"You want some help?" I asked.

"No. I can do it myself," Bobby replied.

"Wait, I want to pet it," cried a little girl named June.

"You don't pet fish," Bobby said with disgust. He threw the fish back into the lake. I laughed in spite of myself as we gathered up the gear and started back toward the hotel.

"Tell you what," I said to the group as we walked. "When we get back, we'll have fish crackers and peanut butter to celebrate our outing." Margaret nodded in agreement.

Bobby skipped along next to me. "You know something?" he said.

"What?" I asked.

"I'm glad you told me the truth about being scared and stuff," he said. "Grown-ups usually pretend they aren't scared, but kids know anyway."

"Bobby," I said, "I have a feeling that you don't miss very much." I ruffled the top of his head, and he smiled.

"Know what? We're going to be here two whole weeks, so I'm probably going to be able to help you out some more," he exclaimed.

"That's great," I told him. "I'm sure we'll have lots of fun."

He was such a cute kid. I hoped that his parents would send him down to the rec room often. I listened in as he told fish jokes while the kids ate their snacks. With Bobby around, things would not be dull.

By the time the last child left that night, I was bone weary from being outdoors all day. After grabbing a sandwich in the cafeteria, I went back to my room. I could hardly wait to sink into a nice hot bath. The thought of putting in lots of bubble bath and soaking for hours seemed absolutely wonderful. Lisa would probably be off somewhere with Bill, and that was just fine with me. I was ready for a self-indulgent, quiet evening. How great it would be just to curl up in my pajamas and start one of the novels I'd brought along. Opening the door, I thought I'd never been so tired.

Then I saw a note on my bed. It said, "Don't forget, there's a party in the grove tonight. Be there as soon as you get off. See you—Lisa."

I'd completely forgotten about the party, and I should have been grateful for the reminder. But all I could do was look longingly at the bathtub. *Oh, well,* I thought, *I have an image to maintain.* After peeling off my uniform, I jumped into the shower. I put on jeans and a sweatshirt. Then I looked in the mirror and yawned. "What's the matter with you, Jill," I said aloud. "How can you be tired? You're going to a great party, all because you're lucky enough to be part of the popular crowd here."

I fluffed up my hair with a brush, put on some lip gloss, and started out the door. Giving my bed one final look and wishing that I could do what I wanted to do instead of what

I had to do, I left the room and headed for the grove. Soon, the sound of music was drifting into the night air. I wondered briefly if Peter would be there, but then I shrugged away the thought. If he *was* there, he'd just spoil my fun.

Todd saw me first. "Hey, Jillian! What took you so long to get here?" he called out. He was standing near the area where people were dancing.

"Want to dance?" he asked.

"Sure," I said. I ignored my aching bones and threw myself into the music. We had danced through three or four songs when Todd motioned me over to a group standing by a big cooler. 'I'm dying of thirst," he yelled over the music. I nodded.

"Hi, guys," Greg said. "You know, I was just thinking that we need to do a little exploring away from the resort. Who's off on Monday?"

"I am," Lisa said. "And so's Jillian."

Several other people called out that they were off, too.

"So what do you have in mind?" asked Lisa.

"The Aerial Tramway. Be there. One o'clock and bring a picnic lunch. One for yourself and one for me," Greg said flippantly.

"You wish," retorted Lisa. Bill was next to her.

"Oh," said Traci, "the Aerial Tram—it's one block away from the post office, and it will take us up to the summit of Prospect Mountain. It's a beautiful view on the way up, and once you've arrived, you can see Longs Peak— and . . . uh . . . and . . ." Traci bit her lip trying to remember. "Oh, shoot! I can't think of the rest of it. I've already failed that dumb employee test once, and if I fail again, I'm dead," she grumbled.

"I know what you mean," Lisa said. "I tried studying for the test, but my brain absolutely refused to absorb the information. I don't think anyone should have to take tests in summer, so I cheated."

"Lisa! How could you cheat?" I asked. The words just slipped out before I could stop them. I mean, I didn't like studying, and I was nervous about taking the test, but this resort was Mr. Scherring's whole life. If the employees didn't want to do things his way, they didn't have to work for him. If a guest asked Lisa any questions about the resort, she wouldn't know the answers. Mr. Scherring's motto of the informed friendliness of the employees wouldn't be worth a thing. I was shocked.

No one seemed to have heard my comment. The conversation was focused on plans for Monday's outing, and everything had been completely settled.

Todd put his arm around my shoulders. "The best thing about that tram is that it's suspended on wires like a ski lift, and it's a long way down to the ground. A girl feels pretty good having someone to lean on while she's up there."

"Hey, Bozo, don't be so sure it's you she's interested in leaning on," Andy said. "Come on, Jillian, let's dance."

I danced with Andy and then with Todd. Once more, they both walked me back toward my room. I had to admit that I was flattered. In spite of my earlier reluctance to go to the party, I was glad I'd gone. It was pretty exhilarating to realize that a month ago, no boy had even been interested in me. Now guys were carrying on a battle for my attention.

I went to bed absolutely exhausted. It took so much concentration being Jillian. I had to be alert and ready for anything.

Lisa came in just as I was drifting off to sleep.

"Did you and Bill have a good time?" I mumbled sleepily.

"He's just the best," she said enthusiastically. "And it's not too shabby that you have both Todd and Andy fighting over which one will get to be with you. Who do you like best, anyway?"

"Oh, I really don't know," I said, rubbing my eyes. I couldn't tell her that the only boy who really interested me wasn't even nice to me.

"Well, it might be fun to string Andy and Todd along this summer," Lisa said. "I don't think either of those guys will give up easily." She had changed into her nightclothes and was getting into bed.

It got quiet in the room, and I assumed that Lisa had drifted off to sleep. Suddenly, she said, "Hey, Jillian, I guess I owe you an apology. I mean about the employee test and stuff."

"Oh, you don't owe me any apology," I said. It was Peter and Mr. Scherring to whom she should apologize. Not that it was any of my business, but I was glad that she was sorry. I considered offering to help her learn the parts she'd cheated on, just in case guests asked her about the resort. But I knew that Jillian wouldn't do that. Weighing my alternatives, I tried to decide whether to just be me or to stay Jillian.

Then Lisa spoke up again. "You know, at first I thought you were serious when you got so huffy about my cheating. Then I realized that you were probably just nervous about the test. You don't have to worry. Nobody watches you that carefully. You won't get caught if you cheat."

I heard her roll over. Cyndi wouldn't have cared about someone cheating, but I did.

Suddenly I was wide awake. It was getting harder and harder to like myself and be popular, too.

Chapter Eight

The next few days passed very quickly. I'd been at the resort for a whole week, and it was time to take the employee exam. It was scheduled for the morning. I walked into the room where the staff meetings were held. It didn't help to tell myself that I'd studied—I was really nervous. There were several other people already sitting down, but I didn't know any of them. Peter handed each of them an exam, lingering at each desk for a moment. *Maybe without the other kids around, he'll let down his guard a little*, I thought. I'd even go halfway. As he handed me the test, I smiled up at him. "Thanks," I said. "I haven't seen you around much. Maybe we could get together and talk about the test over a soda or something when everyone is done taking it."

He stared at me for a minute. "Jillian, either you pass the test or you don't but you do it on your own." he said roughly. Then he went on to the next person. I couldn't believe it! *Peter thought I was trying to get him to give me a good grade,* I fumed. *I'll get a perfect score on his stupid test and prove that I don't need any special favors!* I began to read. The first question was a fill-in-the-blanks: "Estes Park is the gateway to (blank)."

I wrote, "Rocky Mountain National Park." That was really all the question required, but I carefully added, "Rocky Mountain National Park covers 405 square miles that include over 750 species of wild flowers, 215 varieties of birds, and reaches a peak of 13,560 feet above sea level." I'd show that Peter!

So much for that question, I thought smugly. As I continued the test, I gave the most elaborate explanation possible on every question. I spared no details and embellished every answer. I knew the material, and Peter was going to have proof.

Finally, I glanced up and noticed that the room was empty except for Peter.

"If you don't know the stuff," he said coldly, "why don't you quit wasting your time and mine? You can take the test again some other time."

I fought the urge to tell him to get off my back and gave him a big smile instead.

"Is that your answer to everything?" he asked.

I remained silent and went back to my test. If Peter thought I was all smile and no substance, he was in for a surprise. I read the last question: "What is the philosophy of the resort?" I thought again of Lisa. *How could she cheat through the whole thing and still answer that one?* I wrote: "Every employee is a personal ambassador of goodwill and a potential salesperson for the resort."

There were arrows going every which way on my paper because I hadn't had enough space for my answer. My hand hurt from writing, but it was worth it. Peter was going to owe me quite an apology.

I walked up to Peter and thrust the paper into his hand. My hand brushed his as I waited breathlessly for him to look over my test, but he didn't even glance at it. He put my paper on the bottom of the stack and walked out of the room without looking back.

Jerk, I thought to myself, holding back the tears. I wasn't sure whether I meant that *he* was a jerk for the way he acted or that *I* was a jerk for caring—or both.

Three days later, I was resting in my room when Esther, an older woman who was teaching a crafts class at the resort, knocked on my open door. She had an envelope with her. "Peter asked me if I'd mind delivering this to you," she said. I knew it was my test.

"Oh," I said. I'd been counting on his face-to-face apology to me. "Thank you."

"You know," she said, "you look a little upset. Don't be. I'm sure your test is fine. I was scared to death when I took mine." She sat down on my bed and leaned toward me. "You see, Mr. Scherring saw my rock paintings at the Spring Arts Fair in Estes Park. He contacted me, saying I was very good and would I consider giving lessons to some of his guests.

"Why, land sakes, I was flattered. Scherring's Rose of the Rockies is the best place around, and nobody's given me much thought for years. I was thrilled to be offered a job at such a place, and I certainly needed the money. But then I found out about the test," she said. Esther's veined hand fluttered up to straighten her glasses. "Well, I hadn't taken a test in forty years, and I got so scared that I came by to refuse the job. Mr. Scherring was out, and I met Peter. He asked me why I didn't want to work here, and, well, I'm afraid that I sounded a little upset when I told him that I just couldn't take a test at my age. But Peter made me promise to try, and he said he'd help me."

"Peter?" I stuttered.

"Yes, and do you know what that nice young man did? He came by my house in town on his one day off and showed me just how to learn the material," she explained.

Could her "nice young man" be the same person who'd been so nasty to me? It just didn't add up. Esther seemed to take my silence as her cue to leave. She stood up. "I'm afraid I have been running on. It's just so good to be out with people and doing something I love. Bless Mr. Scherring, and bless Peter Wilson," she said.

Esther left, and I turned the envelope over, wishing that Peter had handed it to me personally. Anxiously, I began untwisting the string on the back of the envelope, but before I could get it open, the door crashed open. I jumped to my feet.

"Sorry," Lisa said, "I didn't mean to slam the door. I'm in an incredible hurry. Things got really slow in the restaurant, and Bill's off, so I slipped out for a few minutes to be with him. I didn't want to be too obvious about it, so I left my uniform in here." I watched as she pulled the familiar yellow shirt over her head. Lisa combed her hair and waved as she ran out the door.

I shook my head. I was happy for her that she had a boyfriend. But didn't she think she owed anything to her job at *all*? Pulling my test out of the envelope, I tried to put Lisa and her behavior out of my head. I hoped that Peter would at least have written a nice note on the bottom of my paper.

I pulled the test from the envelope; the word PASSED was neatly printed in green ink at the top of the first page. I flipped through the rest of the test. There were no other marks on it. I went through it again. There was no apology, no word of praise, no anything. I threw the test down on my bed. I'd had it. For the tenth time in one week, I resolved that I didn't care about Peter Wilson. He'd singled me out for his own purposes, and I wasn't going to take it anymore.

Anyway, I didn't need Peter. Andy was a lot of fun, always ready for a joke or a party. And Todd was really quite handsome.

I was too upset to eat at lunchtime, and I was still angry when I got to work. When

Margaret asked me to mix some paint, I snapped at her.

"I always have the supplies ready to use. Haven't you even noticed?" I said.

"Jillian, I was just asking," Margaret protested. "I *do* notice all the work you do around here."

"I'm sorry," I said instantly. "I don't know what's wrong with me." Always pretending to be someone I wasn't *and* dealing with Peter was really taking its toll on me. I couldn't tell Margaret that, so I added, "I guess I'm just a little tired today."

"That's OK," she said. "Don't worry about it. Besides, it's going to be an easy day—we've got a guest teacher coming in."

"Who?" I asked.

"Her name is Esther," Margaret said.

"Oh, I've met her," I said. "She's a terrific lady."

"I made her a deal—we'll get the kids to collect rocks for her classes, and she'll give them a simplified lesson on how to paint them! So we'll take them swimming for an hour, let them dry off, and then we'll go rock hunting. By that time they should be ready to sit down and do something quiet, and you and I can relax while Esther teaches them to rock paint."

At that moment kids began piling into the rec room. They were really wound up, and Bobby ran over to me.

"Are we going fishing again today? I'll help you," he said.

"Not today," I said. "But I think you'll like the things we are doing. We're going to go swimming."

"I'm a good swimmer," Bobby boasted. "You'll see." The kids were eager to get to the swimming pool, and Margaret and I were glad to let them play. I dangled my feet in the water and kept an eye on the kids splashing around.

I noticed a lone swimmer making smooth easy strokes up and down the length of the pool. He swam lap after lap, barely stirring up the water. Bobby came over to me. "Wow," he said, pulling my arm. "Look at that guy! I'm going to ask him to help me with my breaststroke." He marched off toward the end of the pool before I could stop him. I watched as he approached the figure emerging from the pool. "You're great!" Bobby said. "I'm Bobby. Will you show me how to do the breast-stroke?"

I held my breath. It was Peter. If he bit off Bobby's head the way he usually took mine off, I was going to give him a piece of my mind. I didn't care anymore about what Jillian would have done. Bobby was a sweet kid, and he didn't deserve Peter's sarcasm.

I needn't have worried. Peter stuck out his hand. "Hi, Bobby. I'm Peter, and I'm not really that great a swimmer," he said, "but I'll be glad to show you a stroke or two."

Margaret was watching the few kids who were still in the pool, so I kept an eye on Peter and Bobby. Peter was very patient. He made sure that Bobby didn't lose his confidence. "Hey, Bobby, don't get discouraged," Peter told him. "I wasn't nearly as good as you are when I was your age."

"Aw, you're just saying that," Bobby said.

"Hey, I wouldn't kid you. Come on, try that last stroke again," Peter said.

I couldn't get over it. Peter Wilson was, from all my observations, one of the most terrific guys I'd ever met. He was also one of the nastiest people I'd ever encountered. And all I'd ever done was try to make him like me.

I dried off some of the children while Margaret rounded up the others from the pool. From the corner of my eye, I saw Peter looking at me. Quickly, I looked away. When we got back to the rec room, Bobby ran up to me.

"Hey, where did you go?" he asked. "I told

that guy all about you. I wanted him to meet you."

"Thanks," I told Bobby, "I've already met him. But I'm glad you had fun together." *Boy*, I thought, *Peter probably thinks I put Bobby up to that.*

Well, I didn't care. I just didn't have the time—or the heart—to care about Peter Wilson anymore.

Chapter Nine

At the regular staff meeting, I sat in the back of the room so that Peter couldn't even see me. It was a fairly routine meeting, and when it was over, I headed straight for the door. Peter called out to me. "About your test," he said, coming toward me.

"Yes?" I said in my old voice. I caught myself just in time. I turned a radiant smile on him and added, "What about my test, Peter?"

Peter's voice turned cold. "It was a mess. I hope you're neater on the job." He stood there, as if he was waiting for an answer. I turned around and walked away without saying a word. As I was leaving, I heard Peter say to someone, "Hey, I wanted to tell you what great work you did on that banquet last night."

I was furious. It took all my self-control not to run back and tell him off.

"Jill," I heard a male voice call. I ignored him. I was in no mood to be sweet. I was going back to my room before I told Peter off and jeopardized my job. "Jill," he called again. I recognized the voice.

"Hi, Mr. Scherring," I said, smiling.

"I spoke to Margaret the other day, and she told me what a great job you're doing. But then Peter probably already let you know that," he said. "You know, I'm not surprised that you're such a good addition to the summer staff; you're your father's daughter, and he always did things right. I also wanted to ask how you're getting along here?"

"I'm really having a good time, Mr. Scherring. Margaret and the kids are really great," I said.

"That's good. I meant to check on you earlier, but the days just fly by, don't they?" he asked. I nodded, pretending everything was fine. I wanted to tell Mr. Scherring that his boy wonder was the meanest person I'd ever met, but I wasn't sure that anyone except me would ever believe it.

"Well, I'll let you go, Jill. I have to talk to Peter about the Chuck Wagon Bonanza, and now's as good a time as any." Mr. Scherring excused himself, and I went back toward my room. Once more I had managed to keep my anger in check.

Life at the resort fell into a pretty predictable pattern. There were about ten of us who seemed to be the really in-group among the employees. We were the ones who were always planning trips or parties. We danced in the grove every other night and headed into town to go on the water slides, or rent go-carts, or run the miniature trains as often as we could.

Margaret's niece came to visit her at the end of June. She offered to help out in the rec room while she was visiting. It was great to have the extra pair of hands, and she seemed really nice. One night, without even thinking about it, I invited her to one of our parties. She danced with a couple of guys, and I thought she enjoyed herself. But after it was over that night, Lisa asked me not to invite her along again.

"Why not?" I asked. "What did she do?"

"Well," Lisa said, hedging, "she didn't really *do* anything. You're not good friends with her, are you?"

"No. I told you, she's Margaret's niece, and I just met her," I said.

"Good. Then it won't hurt your feelings if I tell you that she's not really our type. She just doesn't quite fit in. I mean, we don't want just anyone at our parties, or they'll be just like any other party. You *know* what I mean," Lisa said, prodding me.

I didn't say anything, but I was thinking that Lisa and her friends probably wouldn't want the *real* me at their parties, either. It was Jillian they liked. It was *that* person who fit in so well with their little group, not me. I sighed. Cyndi would have shrugged off the news that Margaret's niece wouldn't be invited along, but I couldn't.

Lisa mistook my sigh for concern. "Hey, listen, don't feel bad. I mean we all take a chance sometimes. The kids just about *died* when I first suggested bringing you into our group, but it worked out just fine," she told me. Now *that* made me mad. I almost blew it, and let Lisa have a piece of my mind. Instead, I looked indignant, just as I knew Jillian should. "You mean they were considering leaving me out?" I demanded.

"Hey, that's ancient history. Besides, you're the only one of us stringing two guys along at the same time," Lisa said. "That's quite an accomplishment."

Lisa was right—Andy and Todd were available whenever I wanted them around. At first it had been kind of fun, but I knew I wasn't really crazy about either one of them. And I'd found out that they had been friends most of their lives and had been competing over everything for as long as they could remember. Sometimes I had the feeling that not losing to the other guy was more important to them than winning me.

I had begun to get a lot of headaches, and I decided that it was from trying so hard, for so long, to be someone I wasn't. There was no one around with whom I could let down my guard. I'd considered talking to Margaret about it, but I knew that I had really hurt her by dumping her niece. I didn't blame her, either. I didn't like myself very much lately. Somehow I'd gotten caught up in a whirling mess, and I couldn't get out of it.

I couldn't even confide in Angie. Her most recent letter had dashed any hopes I'd had of telling her the whole story. "Dear Jill," she'd written, "I hope you don't mind, but I've been sharing your letters with everyone in the gang. We can hardly wait until we hear from you again. It's even better than anything any of us imagined last spring. It's a good thing that you kept badgering your folks until they gave in. You don't know what any of us would give to be able to trade places with you for one week—even one day would be great. I mean, dangling two guys at the same time? I'm still trying to get David to ask me out for a soda—Dutch treat, even! Please keep writing. Your letters are the best thing about the whole summer."

I had put Angie's letter down and sighed. If I told her all my troubles, she'd think I was crazy. Maybe I was. My summer was everything any girl could have ever hoped for. I'd been accepted by the best crowd, and I had two older guys fighting over me. My job was fun, my roommate was nice enough, and to top it all off, I was in the most beautiful vacation spot in the country. There had to be something wrong with me. Who wouldn't love to be in my position?

I tried to talk to Lisa. Of course, I couldn't mention Cyndi Norwood, but Greg had told me during lunch that Lisa and Peter had gone to the same high school. I thought that maybe she could help me resolve my feelings about him.

One night as she was polishing her toenails, I said, very casually, "I understand you and Peter Wilson go to the same high school in Denver."

"Yes," she replied, concentrating on her toes.

"Well, did you see him much?"

"No, our high school is huge, and I stick to my own little group, if you know what I mean," she replied, looking at the results of one finished foot.

"Too bad. He's pretty good-looking," I commented.

Now that was a subject that interested Lisa. "You know, that's exactly what I thought when I first saw him this summer. But now I don't know. He takes his whole job and responsibility too seriously. I don't think we'd go together too well. Bill thinks he's weird," she said.

I knew I should just let the subject of Peter drop, but I couldn't. If there was one thing Lisa was an expert on, it was boys. I was sure that she could shed a little light on Peter for me, so I steered the conversation back to him again.

"Hey, is Peter going to let you do some waitressing as well as busing?"

"I don't know," she said. "He told me he'd check the schedules. He probably will if he can. He does seem nice enough. You know," she added, "you should ask him if you can make a switch. You don't want to get stuck with those little kids for the whole summer, do you? I think there might be an opening for an assistant salad server in the main restaurant's kitchen."

"Making salads doesn't exactly sound thrilling," I said, laughing to soften the words. Cyndi never liked to sound too serious or critical.

"True," Lisa acknowledged. She shook a bottle of nail polish top coat. "But flirting with the guys who work in the kitchen isn't too boring."

I laughed again. "Maybe I *will* try to switch," I remarked. I knew I wouldn't even consider it. The time I spent working with the little kids was the only time that I'd been really happy at the resort. One rainy day I had even borrowed the resort's video camera and let the kids make their own video. They had planned their costumes, and the set, and made up a song. The video had taken an entire afternoon to film, and then the final four-minute production had been presented at a special evening show to all the parents.

Bobby had called me up to the front to announce to all the parents that I was the person who'd helped them with everything. I'd tried to tell the parents that the kids had done all the work, but I hadn't been able to talk over the applause. All of a sudden I saw Peter's face in the back of the room. I'd had no idea that he'd been there. He was grinning from ear to ear, and he flashed me a sign that meant "A-OK."

I thought that he might mention it to me later, but he never said a word. The next day I asked Margaret if she knew why Peter had come to the performance. She had just shrugged. "I've seen him peeking in the window and watching us a lot. I just thought that it was part of his job," she'd said. I knew that she was right.

"If you don't want to work as a kitchen helper," Lisa went on, "then at least scout out some of the other stations. You know you can observe anywhere," she reminded me.

"You just want me to scout out where the other cute guys in this hotel work," I teased good-naturedly.

"OK, so you're on to me," she said, pouting.

"Listen, Lisa," I said in my perfected Cyndi imitation. "I'm not really complaining. Actually, I'm complimenting you on a great idea."

Lisa smiled. "Now that's what I like to hear."

I finally did set up some observation times at different places around the hotel. I figured that even if I never came back, I might as well find out as much as I could while I was there. I didn't like anything about food preparation, and since I hated cleaning even my own room, maid service was also out.

But working at the front desk sounded absolutely fascinating. I observed what went on a few times. People checked in and out, asked a thousand questions, changed rooms, extended or shortened their stays, and in spite of everything, the employees at the front desk never seemed to get ruffled.

Several times, as I wandered around the resort, I saw Peter with other employees. He was always kind and gentle. But his rudeness to me never faltered. If anything, it became more apparent, even to casual observers. At our staff meetings, Peter had always made a point of singling out those employees who he felt had done an especially good job—and those whose work needed improvement. Peter frequently had something negative to say about my performance. Andy finally asked me if I had some kind of problem with Peter. I just laughed, batted my eyelashes, and said, "Why, Andy, I've got my hands full with you, don't you think?"

He grinned. "Then why don't we hit the water slide tomorrow?" he suggested.

Todd sauntered up to us.

"Oh, are we all going someplace?" he asked.

"No, *we* are not!" Andy said. "Jillian and I—"

"Hey, guys," Todd yelled to Traci and two other girls. "Who's up for the water slide tomorrow?" In no time we had a few kids around us making plans. Quite honestly, I was glad we were going as a group. Andy had been getting really affectionate lately, and it was just easier if there was a crowd around. Todd looked smug at having cut in on my date with Andy, and Andy glowered at him.

"You know, Jillian, we could always sneak off and do something else—just the two of us," Andy whispered.

I gave him my best Cyndi look. "Oh, Andy, there's no need to do that. It would just make everyone think we didn't like them. Besides, when I'm with you I don't even notice anyone else." The words sounded unbelievably phony to me, but somehow, with the right voice and manner, Andy just accepted it.

When Andy turned away from me to talk to someone else, I walked by Todd and smiled warmly. "I'm really glad you're going to be at the water slide tomorrow," I said.

He grinned. "Me, too. Now we just have to get rid of everyone else."

I laughed. "You're terrible. See *you* there," I said.

Andy and Todd both had to rush to work from the staff meeting, so I didn't have to worry about manipulating them anymore. Sometimes, when I was Jillian, I almost felt as if I were standing outside myself—watching an actress. But her methods sure worked.

I was still thinking about that when Peter walked out of the staff room. I had promised myself that I'd never speak to Peter again, and I'd meant it. But for some reason, it hit me as he walked by that if Jillian's methods worked on everyone else, they'd eventually work on Peter, too; maybe I just hadn't tried hard enough. "Peter, we're all going to the water slide in town tomorrow," I said. I looked at him with Cyndi's most admiring gaze. "We're leaving around one, and if you can make it, please join us."

Peter gave me a cool stare, and I could feel my face flushing as his deep blue eyes looked searchingly into mine. "OK," he said slowly. "I'll be there."

Chapter Ten

I was so nervous that night that I could hardly sleep. Maybe things were finally going to click between Peter and me. I had to talk to someone about my feelings, so when Lisa came in, I casually mentioned that she'd never believe who was joining us in town the next day.

"Try me," she said, climbing into her bed.

"Peter Wilson," I replied, trying to make sure the way I felt about him didn't show in my voice.

Lisa sat up and leaned on one elbow. "You invited him after the way he's treated you? You're a nicer person than I am, that's all I can say." Then she began to smile. "Oh, I see. You're pretty clever. This way you can check out Peter's handsome face, and if nothing works out, you'll still have Andy and Todd there to hang out with. Now that's a girl who thinks ahead."

"No, that's not really what I meant at all," I tried to explain, sorry that I'd even started the conversation in the first place. Jillian wouldn't admit that she had a tremendous crush on a boy who seemed to hate her. "I've decided that I need a new challenge," I said. Lisa seemed to accept that, and we went to sleep.

The day at the water slides was exhausting. While we were waiting for everyone to get there so we could leave, I had to try not to keep my eyes glued to the door to see if Peter was actually coming. He finally arrived—the last one. But then I didn't know which was harder, acting as if I didn't care who walked through the door, or trying to hide how happy I was once he'd arrived.

There was also the challenge of riding in the Jeep Peter was in. I failed at that one; Andy was driving one of the other Jeeps, and he called out that he'd saved me a seat.

The biggest challenge of the day, however, came when we arrived at the slides. Peter spent the entire day laughing, swimming, and talking to almost everyone *except* me. If I could have just gone home, I would have. But, since I couldn't, I had to pretend I was having a good time and stick it out for the afternoon.

By the time we got back to the hotel that night, my head was throbbing. I simply had to forget about Peter, because if I didn't, there would be many more wasted afternoons and splitting headaches. I knew that Cyndi would have written Peter off long ago and just sat back and thoroughly enjoyed everyone else's attention. *But I'm not Cyndi,* I thought. *And I'm sick and tired of pretending.*

I dismissed that thought from my mind. *You're just a little depressed about Peter,* I told myself. I'd been envious of Cyndi's popularity for years; now I was actually getting to live her life for a summer. How could that be anything but great?

The time passed, and there were new children to greet and entertain each day. The staff was preparing for an event called the Chuck Wagon Bonanza, which would be held on the third weekend in July. Mr. Scherring put it on every year, and Peter said that the event not only drew guests from the resort, but many people from Estes Park and the surrounding area as well. People even drove up from Denver each year for the event.

"Some of you will be pulling extra duty the week before the Chuck Wagon Bonanza so we can make sure we're ready," Peter had announced at a staff meeting. "I'll try to spread the work out as evenly as possible." I figured he meant food servers and some of the other employees. It didn't sound as if it would make any difference in the children's activities program, so I didn't pay much attention to exact times or dates.

Meanwhile, I made certain that I was never around Peter unless we were at staff meetings. I could never make myself dislike him, but I made sure I kept my distance. We'd had a full house of kids in the rec room almost every day, and keeping up with them usually left me too tired to do much else, so staying out of Peter's way wasn't very hard. I'd been so exhausted lately that I'd been going straight to bed after work, missing some of the parties in the grove. It seemed like such a long time ago when that first one had been so important to me.

But going to bed early had its rewards. I woke up well before it was time to be at work, so I could spend time walking around among the pine trees, or down by the lake. I loved the solitude, and it was a tremendous relief not to worry about what I was going to say to whom. Those mornings refreshed me and made the summer special.

I was passing by the main entrance one day and decided to stop in and observe things at the registration desk. I hadn't been there for a while, and it had always seemed very interesting.

When I walked up to the counter in the lobby, a harried-looking older man behind the desk spotted me and said, "Ah, you must be Sally's replacement. I'm so glad you're here. Not only are we a person short, but I ate something that has made me terribly ill. I'll try to be back in a few minutes."

"Wait," I said in panic as he started to leave, "I'm just here to observe. I'd be glad to help, but I'm not really sure I know what I'm supposed to do."

Clutching at his stomach, the man explained, "It's easy. Everything's logical. Besides, I'm sure Sally's replacement will be here any minute. Just try your best to look as if you know what you're doing, and you'll be fine." Then he hurried off.

I stood behind the desk, staring at the reservations computer and praying that no one would come up to me. A young couple approached me, and I held my breath. But it turned out that all they wanted to know was if I could give them some information about Estes Park.

Smiling with relief, I told them in detail about the shops, restaurants, and the entertainment. They were very appreciative, and I started feeling more confident.

My confidence didn't last long, though. A man wearing a dark suit stomped up to the counter. "I'd like to check in," he barked.

"Check in?" I said pleasantly. "I'm just filling in for someone for a minute. Would you mind waiting a moment?"

"Let me explain something to you, young lady," the man said. "I missed my plane from New York, so I had to take another flight that made three stops before getting to Denver. Then I had to rent a car to drive here from Denver, because the people who were supposed to meet me had already left. I've been traveling for eleven hours. Right now I'm extremely tired, not very happy, and ready to get to my room and sleep. Do I make myself clear?"

I searched the lobby for another reservations employee, but there wasn't even a bellboy nearby. The only other staff people in the lobby just then were the two women in the cashier's cage, and they had a long line of people waiting for them.

Maybe I should call up to the main office, I thought. Mr. Scherring would know what to do. I picked up the phone as the man glared at me. "Now what's the problem?" he asked. His face was red with anger.

"I'll just be a minute, sir," I said, scanning the phone list for the extension in Mr. Scherring's office. Suddenly it occurred to me that Peter might answer. I put the phone down and stared at the reservations computer. How hard could it be? Everything was labeled.

"All right, sir, I'm so sorry for the delay. I'll get you your room right now. Your name?"

He said, "Smith! Wallace Smith."

I punched his name into the computer, followed the directions on the screen, and in a couple of minutes, the printer produced a reservation card. It read: SMITH. WALLACE C. So far, so good. I knew he was supposed to sign something, but I wasn't sure if this was it. I also didn't know where the key to the room was kept.

Well, I decided, *if this isn't the right form for him to sign, they can always have him sign another one later. At least we'll have kept a guest happy by getting him promptly to his room.* Even Peter couldn't have argued with that.

Mr. Smith signed the sheet. He looked

around the lobby and, seeing no bellboy, said, "My luggage is in the dark brown Datsun outside. Have one of your people bring it to my room—here are the car keys. I'll just take the room key and head upstairs now."

"The key?" I said. I looked around frantically, wondering where the keys were.

"Behind you, in the mailbox!" Mr. Smith barked.

"Of course, sir," I said, smiling. How dumb of me to forget that the extra room keys were kept in the mailbox! I handed him a key. "I hope you enjoy your stay at Scherring's," I said.

Minutes later a girl arrived who said she was Sally's replacement. Then the older gentleman, Mr. Compton, returned. I was glad to see both of them and told them what I had done. Mr. Compton nodded and said it sounded as though I'd done just the right thing. Suddenly there was a rush at the reservations desk, and both he and Sally were too busy to talk to me. I watched them, feeling grateful that I hadn't had to contend with so many people crowding around the desk when I'd been there alone.

The lobby was still busy, when I heard a familiar voice shouting, "What kind of place is this, anyway?" It was Mr. Smith. I felt a horrible thud in the pit of my stomach.

Mr. Smith's voice boomed through the lobby, and Peter was next to him in a matter of seconds. The man was so angry that not only was his face still red, but he was also shaking. Peter persuaded him to stop shouting, but as they approached the reservation desk, Mr. Smith pointed to me with angry gestures. I wanted to run away, but my legs felt wooden and I couldn't move.

Peter reached the counter and called Mr. Compton over. "It seems that we have mistakenly given Mr. Smith a room that was already occupied. When he opened the door, the guest in the room became quite angry with him. Naturally Mr. Smith is a little upset over the incident. I've offered him our apologies. Would you please see that he gets a room immediately, and to make up for our mistake, please charge him half the regular price for it," he explained.

Mr. Compton hastily accommodated the request, and Peter personally accompanied the man to his new room. After they left, Mr. Compton asked me how on earth I'd managed to give Mr. Smith an occupied room. I shrugged and showed him what I had done.

"OK," he said, watching me. "You were doing just fine until you forgot to check for other Wallace Smiths. It's an incredible coincidence, but we've already got one Wallace Smith checked in, and you didn't tell the computer that this was another person."

Peter arrived back at the registration desk in time to hear Mr. Compton's explanation. Mr. Compton told him that he had asked me to take over for a few minutes because he hadn't been feeling well, and he apologized.

"It's not your fault," Peter reassured him. "Jillian checked Mr. Smith in, didn't she?" he asked.

"Yes, but as I told you, I left so suddenly. It was really my fault," Mr. Compton said.

"I understand," Peter said abruptly, cutting Mr. Compton off. "But your only mistake was in assuming that there was anything like a brain behind Jillian Novick's charming, phony smile. Are you sure that you feel OK now?" he asked. The older man nodded.

Confident that the registration desk was in order, Peter strode back toward the offices. I stood there helplessly for a moment, but then anger began to flood through my whole body. I could feel it moving like a fire from the top of my head to the bottom of my feet. *No one* was going to talk to *me* like that.

I began to head purposefully toward the office where Peter had gone. As I went, it crossed my mind that Cyndi would never do what I was about to do. Cyndi would get even, sooner or later, but she'd never yell at a boy. But what Peter had done had humiliated me too much for me to worry about what anyone else would do. I strode angrily into the office.

I don't know what I would have done if Mr. Scherring had been there. Maybe I would have told Mr. Scherring exactly what was going on, and he'd have to let Peter know that I really *was* doing a good job. But Mr. Scherring wasn't there. Patty, his secretary, asked if she could help me.

"No, uh, I guess I was—"

I didn't have to finish my sentence. A buzzer on her desk went off. "Could you hold on just a minute? I've got to get something down the hall," she said. Just as she left the office, Peter came in through another door.

"Patty, I really appreciate your typing . . ." he started to say. Then he saw that I was there, not Patty. "What now?" he said. "Haven't you caused enough trouble for one day?"

I heard my voice come out clear and strong. "Well, you don't have to worry about my causing any more trouble this summer, because I came in to tell you two things. One: you are the most stuck-up, rude, uncaring person I've ever met. And, two: I quit!"

"Well, that figures," he said. "We have only three days until the biggest event the resort puts on all year, and you quit. Obviously you didn't hear how important the Chuck Wagon Bonanza is. We discussed it in the last five staff meetings, but it's hard to gossip with your friends *and* listen. Obviously you don't know that we've got two girls out sick during the week when we desperately need every employee we've got. Then again, maybe you don't care. Knowing you, I'd guess *that's* it."

"Hold on just one minute," I shouted. "Knowing me? You don't know me at all. I'm not at all like what you think I am. I've been one big fake all summer so I could fit in with everyone, but I have had it." I looked him in the eye. "I'll stay until your dumb Chuck Wagon Bonanza is over, and I'll do a good job just as you *know* I've done all summer. I was only trying to help out this morning, and maybe I didn't do everything right, but at least I *tried* to get a tired guest into his room. And even if I did mess things up, it doesn't excuse your rude behavior. Look, Peter," I said, calming down a little. "I'll do whatever you think I can do to make the resort's Chuck Wagon Bonanza a success, but as of Monday, I've officially quit. As of this moment, you can forget about seeing the smiling, bubbly girl who's been here so far. My name is Jill—just Jill. I'm just plain old boring Jill Novick. See how you like *that*."

I turned on my heel and ran out of the office. As soon as I got back to my room, I cried until there were no more tears left. Then I went to the bathroom and looked in the mirror. A girl with a red nose and eyes so swollen that they were barely open stared back at me. I had to report to work in the rec room in just twenty minutes, and unless I wanted to scare the kids, I had to do something about my appearance. I'd miss lunch, but I didn't care. Putting a cold cloth over my face, I tried to collect my thoughts.

Cyndi would never have confronted Peter that way. Now I'd have to leave my job, and go home a failure. Still, I was glad I had told Peter off. I loved working at Scherrings, but I was sick of being two people.

I dug out the worn red notebook and tore each page into a hundred pieces. I'd had such wonderful plans for a perfect summer, and I'd almost succeeded. But it wasn't worth it. I'd tried to have a perfect summer, but I'd almost lost myself in the process.

Chapter Eleven

"Surprise!" called Bobby when I arrived at the children's rec room. "We came back for the Chuck Wagon Bonanza."

"Well, good afternoon," I said. Bobby's family had wound up their vacation a week earlier. I guess Peter was right—people did drive up from Denver for the event.

Bobby's earnest eyes looked at me from his freckled face. "I can hardly wait for the Chuck Wagon Bonanza, can you? Do you know the guy who is doing the roping? Will you introduce me? Do you think he'll teach me how?" he asked.

I hated to burst Bobby's bubble, but I'd been so distracted by other things, that I'd hardly paid any attention to the preparations for the Chuck Wagon Bonanza. I'd either been trying to avoid Peter, or I'd affected the same detached attitude toward it that Lisa had. She and Andy had complained that it was one less day for them to party. Quickly, I searched my memory just to dredge up something to say about it. "It will be out in the grove," I began. "Everything will be western, from the roping and riding to a real cowboy barbecue." I couldn't remember much else. I could tell him about the big campfire, and the dance, and that it was the biggest event of the season, but Bobby already knew all that. Disappointed by my silence, he ran off to be with the other kids.

Margaret and I took them on a scavenger hunt we'd planned outside, and I watched the kids scramble around for the items on their lists for a while. But my thoughts kept wandering. I was leaving Scherring's in a few days, and I would miss being there very much. It was strange how, in spite of all my careful planning for the summer, nothing had turned out right at all.

I checked the special-duty lists on the way home from work that evening, and it said that I was scheduled to help with the "final site inspection" at seven-thirty the next morning. Even though I had no idea what "final site inspection" entailed, I did know one thing: I wasn't taking any grief from Peter Wilson about the way I did it.

I got back to my room and flopped on my bed, and then I noticed that Lisa had left me a note telling me to go to the small grove for a party. I crinkled it up and threw it in the wastebasket. "That was the other me," I said aloud. "I'm pretty sure the real me wouldn't fit in with that group."

I didn't even feel sorry about that. I just felt relieved. Those kids hadn't been nearly as much fun once I was a part of their group as they had appeared when I was an outsider. I wondered if the same were true of Cyndi's group at home. We had always just assumed that since they were the most popular, they were also more fun to be with. But suddenly I wondered if they really were so great after all.

Thinking about the site inspection, I wondered if I'd get a chance to talk to some of the other staff members. There were probably some pretty nice kids there, even some who'd like me just the way I was. I'd just been so wrapped up in Lisa's group that I hadn't really met anyone else. Then I reminded myself that it was really too late. As of Monday, I would be gone.

When I woke up the next morning, Lisa was already up and getting dressed to go to work. She seemed surprised to see me awake so early, and I explained that I had to be at a site inspection.

"That explains why you missed our spectacular party at the grove last night," she said. "You know, you'd better watch it. There are lots of other people here who'd love to be invited to our parties. You miss too many, and one of them might take your place." She said it jokingly, but the message was clear. If I'd been deemed cool enough to be invited, I'd better not slight the honor.

"Well," I said, shrugging, "I don't really like going to parties that I'm *required* to attend. You can invite anyone you want in my place, Lisa."

She stared at me but didn't say a word. It was obvious that I'd shocked her.

I ran a brush through my hair and pulled on an old pair of jeans and a T-shirt. Then I rummaged around in my drawer for a clean pair of socks and got out my favorite sneakers.

"You're not going out like *that*, are you?" Lisa asked. "What's with you, anyway?"

"I've got to sit in the back of an open Jeep going down dirt paths. I'll be fine," I said. I left the room and walked toward the Jeep shed, wondering how many of us were doing site inspection.

When I got to the Jeep shed, there was no one else there. I thought at first that maybe I was just early, but then a thought struck me. If this was Peter Wilson's idea of a joke, I'd report him to Mr. Scherring. I really would.

"Hi. Glad to see you're on time," Peter called as he approached me. "Sorry I'm late."

"Where is everyone else?" I asked.

"It's just you and me," he said. There was a wary look in his eyes. "All the set-up work was done yesterday, and we had a large crew for that. Here's a list of everything we need to check; I really think two people can handle it, don't you?"

I looked at the list. Two people could handle it easily. The question was—could Peter and I handle it together? The tension between us was tangible.

We climbed into the Jeep, and Peter started it. The ride out to the Chuck Wagon Bonanza site started off in silence. It was all so ironic,

I thought. I'd have given anything in the weeks before to be out riding in these beautiful mountains with Peter. But now that we were finally together, it was just too late. I felt so stiff and uncomfortable that all I wanted was to get the job finished quickly. This assignment was probably Peter's last test to see if I'd stick to my word about working until I left. Well, I *would*. Still, I bet Peter wished that he were out there with someone else right then. What I wished was that our relationship was the one I'd dreamed we'd have. Then this whole ordeal would have been different.

When we arrived, Peter stopped the Jeep, and we got out. "Do you like it?" he asked me. He sounded unsure of himself.

"It looks wonderful," I said softly. The clearing looked like one gigantic open-air dining hall. There was a real wagon train—four covered wagons lined up like those in a movie set. Peter said that the food would be served from them. There were also about a hundred picnic tables that had been covered with red-and white-checked tablecloths. Benches were placed alongside them. Three stages had been set up over to one side with painted backdrops behind them. One said "Saloon," another said "Dance Hall," and the third said "Old West Theater."

"Let's split the list down the middle," Peter said. "I'll take the first half, you take the second. Then we can switch and check each other's work. It may seem unnecessary, but last year two power cords were left behind. We had to delay our western show while someone went back to the hotel to get them. With a thousand people signed up to attend, we'd like everything to go smoothly this year."

We worked silently for an hour. Then we exchanged lists and went back to work.

"OK, that should do it," Peter finally called. We walked toward the Jeep. I hadn't spoken a word to him in the whole two hours. "Thanks for your help," he said, smiling.

I didn't look at him. There was no point in his being nice now. It was too late; everything was ruined. Just another few minutes in the Jeep, and then I would be safely away from Peter, before he could stir up my feelings for him again.

I sat down in the passenger seat, and he slid into the driver's seat. Peter put the key in the ignition and turned it. Nothing happened.

"Don't worry," he reassured me. "Sometimes this sticks a little."

But after a few minutes, Peter began to look worried. Getting out of the Jeep, he lifted the hood and began tinkering with the engine.

"When I say 'now,'" he called out to me, "try to start it." I did just as he asked, but still nothing happened. Ten more minutes passed before Peter stood up with a defeated look on his face. "I'm really sorry, but I can't get it to start. I guess we'll have to walk back," he said. He had a big smudge of grease across his nose, and I couldn't help feeling sorry for him.

We started to walk. "I can't believe it," he said, obviously angry at himself. "I thought I had everything figured out, but I never planned on the dumb Jeep breaking down. I really feel bad about making you walk all the way back."

To my surprise, I found myself saying, "Oh, that's OK." Cyndi might have thought that there was still a way to flirt with Peter, but I was through with trying to be like her. It had only made me miserable. No, like it or not, I'd decided to just be myself. And since I could never interest a boy like Peter on my own, I figured that there was no point in worrying about it. "I take a lot of long hikes by myself,"

148

I admitted. "Lately, I find it helps me clear my head."

"Yeah," Peter said, "I've been wrestling with some pretty tough questions myself this summer."

I remained silent. A week ago I would have said something provocative—something to get Peter's attention. But just then, I felt like listening.

"A couple of weeks ago," Peter continued, "one of the children disappeared from a group that had gone horseback riding. One minute she was on her horse on the trail, and the next minute both she and the horse were gone. We combed the grounds for nearly an hour before one of the stable hands came riding out. She'd ridden back to the hotel and was bugging the employees to let her feed the other horses. No one knows just how she got back without anyone seeing her, but she did."

I laughed out loud. I was pretty sure I knew which little girl had done that. Her name was Emma, and she'd been a handful for Margaret and me, too.

Peter looked at me and smiled. "That's better. It's good to see you smile." Then he looked down at the ground again. "Anyway, you have no idea how scared I was. I mean, I had this picture in my head of my going to jail for neglect or something."

"But it wasn't your fault," I protested. "No one would have blamed you if something terrible had happened."

"I know, I know. But at the time, it sounded reasonable," he said.

My heart went out to Peter. I knew just what it was like to be blamed for something you hadn't done. Suddenly I wondered if Peter was trying to apologize—to say that he knew that he'd been wrong about me. But if he was, why now?

The resort was coming into view. "The only thing I dislike about my job," Peter continued, "is that I'm never alone. I really thought I'd be able to spend a lot more time hiking this year—getting away from everything—but I haven't had a moment to myself."

"I'd miss that," I said. "I've started taking long walks in the morning. I feel totally relaxed within minutes. And having time alone with your thoughts really helps you sort things out. It's my favorite time of the day," I finished. Briefly, I wondered if Peter would think I was being antisocial, or that I didn't like the people at Scherring's. But then, somehow, I knew that he'd understand what I meant.

"I guess my favorite part of the day, when they're scheduled, is the staff meetings. I feel like it's my chance to check in with everyone, to make sure everything's OK." He paused. "You know, it's funny but I used to hate staff meetings. I didn't like standing up in front of everyone and telling them what to do," he admitted. "I guess I've just learned how to handle that part of my job better."

I was thinking of how I'd come to despise staff meetings because of Peter. *Forget it, Jill,* I told myself. I didn't have the energy to get mad anymore.

"Of course, I'm still learning how to handle things," Peter said. "I really blew a situation the other day. An employee gave out the wrong room reservation—an honest mistake—and I was pretty hard on her. I owe her a big apology."

We were almost back at the hotel. I didn't know what to say. Perhaps he was just trying to make sure that I didn't really quit—after all, that was his job. But maybe, just *maybe*, he really was sincere.

Suddenly Peter turned to me. "You were a really good sport about having to walk, and I'm sorry about the Jeep. If you were staying on, I'd schedule some extra free time for you. This took up your whole morning."

"Don't worry about it, Peter. It was just one of those things that happens," I said. "It's all right." I looked into his eyes.

"Peter," Patty called from the main entrance to the hotel. "I'm so glad you're back. You've got about a dozen messages that need to be taken care of immediately."

"I'm coming," he called. Then he turned back to me. "Well, I hope you have a good day."

Watching him walk down the lobby hallway, I realized two things. First of all, I never should have quit. I wanted to stay at Scherring's—the place was beautiful, and my job was fun. The second thing, which was harder to admit, was that I was still crazy about Peter Wilson. I didn't understand why, but it was true.

And there was nothing I could do about either revelation. After I'd made such a forceful show of leaving, I couldn't just change my mind. And anyway, no one had asked me to reconsider my decision. As for my feelings about Peter, well, I'd probably never see him again. He was going to be busy all day with last-minute details for the Chuck Wagon Bonanza, and then I'd leave. Besides, just because he was suddenly being nice to me didn't mean that he necessarily liked me. It just meant that he didn't hate me anymore. Maybe he'd even relaxed around me because he knew that I was leaving. I didn't like being suspicious of people, but again I wondered if Peter had only been nice to me so the resort wouldn't end up short an employee until they found a replacement for me.

Chapter Twelve

The next morning—the day of the Chuck Wagon Bonanza—dawned clear and beautiful. A storm had been predicted for the morning, but there was no sign of it. Every job that was not absolutely essential to the hotel had been suspended for the day, so that the staff could be on hand to greet and organize the crowd and to make sure that everyone found his or her way to the bonanza site. I was assigned to work at the information desk in the front lobby along with several other employees.

I got up and dressed quickly in my uniform. Before going to the lobby, I stopped in the employee cafeteria and grabbed a glass of juice and a doughnut. When I arrived at the temporary information desk they'd set up, a girl named Bonnie greeted me.

"Put on one of these cowboy hats. Here are the maps to the site, and over there are some activity lists. They give the times and locations for each event," she said.

"Looks easy," I commented.

She grinned at me. "It is—until you get five people asking you five different questions all at the same time."

Just then, a harried woman approached me with two children hanging onto her skirt. "Are there bathrooms at the Chuck Wagon Bonanza site?" she asked.

"Yes," I said, handing her a map. I pointed out the locations of the rest rooms.

"Did we miss the steer roping?" an old man asked. His wife smiled at me.

"No," I replied. "The Old West steer roping isn't until four-thirty, and the Indian dancing should start at five-thirty." Bonnie was handling people, too, but soon everyone became a blur. I'd answered the same questions so many times that I felt like a robot. But the crowds just kept getting larger. At lunchtime, someone delivered sandwiches and sodas. We had to keep talking to people between bites.

Finally, late in the afternoon, Bonnie asked, "Are you working on the serving line tonight?"

"Yes, why?"

"Then you'd better get down to the Jeep barn. The line doesn't look too bad anymore, anyway. I can handle it from here."

I looked at my watch and realized how late it was. After practically running down to the barn, I hopped on the nearest Jeep. Fortunately, the other staff members with me were also on the serving line, so I knew I wasn't too late.

I'd had nothing to do with the food service since I'd been at Scherring's, so I was a little bit nervous about doing a good job. The other kids in the Jeep assured me that it wasn't too tough. When we arrived at the site, it was hard to believe that it was the same place Peter and I had visited the day before. I looked around in amazement. Although a lot of people were already there, a big hay wagon pulled up and more excited guests climbed off and joined the crowd. Mr. Scherring had arranged the hay-wagon transportation for people who really wanted to get into the spirit of things. The hay wagon left immediately to pick up another group. The Chuck Wagon Bonanza already looked like a huge success.

There were performers on each stage, and

large crowds gathered around them to watch the various shows. I remembered how empty the grounds had looked when we'd checked the site, and it was hard to believe that this was the same place. I automatically scanned the crowd looking for Peter, but I didn't see him.

I walked over to the chuck wagons, which were loaded down with food. Approaching another employee I'd met in the kitchen, I said, "I think I'm supposed to be working here."

He checked a list. "Jillian . . . you're serving beans. Give everyone one large spoonful unless they ask for more." I worked my way down the wagons until I found the one with beans on it. Food service would begin in ten minutes and would last for several hours. My wagon had beans and salad, the next had rolls and desserts; yet another had coffee, sodas, and juices. I checked my watch. People were already getting their plates and lining up. I hoped that whoever was going to serve the salad would show up soon.

The loudspeaker crackled, "Ladies and Gentlemen, in just two minutes we'll start our old-fashioned western barbecue. We'll be serving dinner for three hours, and there's plenty of food, so mosey on over whenever you get hungry," Mr. Scherring said.

Just as the first person started down the buffet line, the salad server slipped into place. "Peter!" I said, unable to keep the surprise out of my voice.

"I almost didn't make it. Isn't this great?" he said. His warm, deep voice was enthusiastic. "This is the most elaborate program and the biggest turnout we've ever had!"

During dinner I kept sneaking peeks at him out of the corner of my eye. His tanned face made his eyes look even bluer, and he was wearing a cowboy hat, tipped slightly to the side, that made him look just a little daring. He was also wearing some kind of after-shave that smelled terrific. For a minute, I felt a little sad. Jillian—or Cyndi—hadn't been able to steal his heart, but I didn't think I could either. And even though I knew I shouldn't have tried to be someone I wasn't, the festive atmosphere and starry night made me wish I was just different enough from the real me to win Peter's love.

But it was too late for that. I would just have to be content to stand beside him for one night and watch as he joked with the guests and handed out salad. At that moment, I didn't care if I spooned out baked beans forever, as long as Peter was next to me.

Every so often, someone would come by with huge, fresh trays of food and take away our empty ones. My whole arm and wrist hurt from hours of scooping, but it seemed like a small price to pay. When the lines were almost gone, Peter turned toward me. "Jillian," he began hesitantly, "do you remember when you were so mad the other day?"

I took a deep breath. "Yes, I remember."

"What did you mean about not being yourself?" he asked.

If I could have invented a good story, I might have. But I was so stunned by his question that all I could do was tell him the truth. "There's this girl at home in San Diego named Cyndi Norwood. She's always been really popular and good at fitting in with people she doesn't know. She has a way of making people want to be her friend. I just thought her personality was probably better than mine, so I tried to borrow it for the summer."

I waited for Peter to say something, but he was suddenly very busy arranging the salad and serving the few people who were still coming through the line. Mr. Scherring announced over the loudspeaker: "Dinner will close in five minutes. If you'd like seconds, thirds, or even cowboy fourths, now's the time to head back to the chuck wagon. We hope you've enjoyed the roping, dancing, and other demonstrations. Now it's your turn to participate. We're going to have ourselves an old-fashioned square dance. And don't any of you worry if you've never square danced before—we'll have you sashaying like a pro before the night is out."

A professional square dance caller walked onto the stage, and a fiddle band set themselves up behind him. I didn't really think many people would join in, despite Mr. Scherring's words of encouragement. After all, the tourists wouldn't know the first thing about square dancing, and neither did I. In fact, I'd only seen it done once before, and it looked as if you had to know what you were doing.

But to my surprise, as the fiddlers started up, square after square of people took the floor. "Come on," yelled the caller. "I want to see *everyone* dancing." I found myself tapping my foot to the music and watching as more people grabbed a partner and followed the caller in the dance. The food was taken away, and a group of boys pushed the chuck wagons back farther to make more room for dancing.

In the midst of the crowd, I saw Lisa, Andy, and Todd dancing along with the rest of their group. They'd made fun of the whole bonanza, calling it corny and stupid. They had also resented having to do the extra work it had required, but now they were out having a great time. I watched as Bill slid his arm around Lisa. Closing my eyes for a minute, I imagined what it would have been like to have Peter put his arm around me like that.

Then I heard Peter say, "Come on, let's dance." He put his hand on my shoulder. I gasped with surprise as I looked up at him. He smiled back down at me. "Don't you want to dance with me?"

At that moment, if I'd learned anything in the whole world from imitating Cyndi, I should have used it. Instead, I swallowed and said in a lame voice, "Uh, aren't we supposed to be working right now?"

"Hey, I thought I was the one who worked all the time," Peter said.

I blushed.

"Come on," he urged.

Blind panic set in at the thought of dancing with Peter. My hands started to sweat. "I can't," I blurted out. "I don't know how to square dance."

"Me, either," he said, laughing. "And neither do the rest of these people."

Almost as if I were in a dream, I felt myself being pulled into one of the squares, and then Peter's arm went around my waist. I was so happy that I felt dizzy. Between listening to what the caller was saying and saving enough breath so that I wouldn't collapse from the exercise, I didn't have time to worry about anything else. I didn't even try to make conversation with Peter. I just let some of the happiness in my heart spill out through the smile on my lips and hoped that the night would never, ever end.

The music did eventually stop. People had begun to leave even before that, and the site had cleared out quickly. Peter suddenly hurried off, without even saying, "It was fun," or "Thanks for the dance," or *anything*.

Sitting down on a log, I thought about the evening. Despite his fast exit, despite the fact that Peter had probably just wanted to dance and I was the only partner he could find, I knew I'd never forget that night. I had never enjoyed dancing with another boy the way I had loved dancing with Peter. Nor had I ever felt the way I had when he took my hand. I stared up at the star-filled sky. There was no point in being in the first staff Jeep back to the resort. That night was my own—for memories, for wishful thinking. I would have to call my parents the next day to tell them I was coming home, and I'd have to get ready to leave.

Suddenly it occurred to me that Mr. Scherring hadn't mentioned my leaving. I wondered if it was because he was too busy with the Chuck Wagon Bonanza to concern himself with me, or if Peter just hadn't told him yet.

I walked toward the loading area.

Big trucks had taken away the more valuable equipment, including the generator that had run the lights. The staff Jeeps had already made several runs back and forth, and there weren't many of us left now. I had to let go of the night, I decided. But just as I climbed into a Jeep, another Jeep drove up. "Uh, Jillian, would you mind working on a final site-cleaning checklist?" Peter called from the driver's seat.

As tired as I was, I was in no hurry to get back to the resort. Even in the semidarkness, Peter's face looked rugged and handsome. Was he leaving then or would he also be working on this final site-cleaning checklist? I wondered. But I couldn't bring myself to ask. I just said, "No problem. I don't mind."

"Good." Peter parked his Jeep and turned to the driver of the other one. "Go ahead. Jill and I will finish up."

The other Jeep took off, and as the sound of its motor died away, I realized that Peter and I were alone. The silence was unsettling, and I was sure that even in the darkness he could see me blush. "So," I said, ignoring the pounding of my heart, "what do we do first?"

"Well, first . . ." he began. He cleared his throat and dug the toe of his sneaker into the dirt. "Uh—I guess that first, I should tell you that I'm really sorry about giving you such a hard time this summer."

"It's OK," I said, deliberately keeping my voice level. *He is a nice person,* I told myself. *He's apologizing because he's nice. You don't matter to him.* I had to keep repeating that to myself so it wouldn't hurt.

We both stood there in silence for a moment. "Well, let's see," Peter said. His voice had an authoritative air. "We'd better check to make sure that the generator is covered."

"The truck took that back a few minutes ago," I replied.

"Oh, well," Peter began to sound flustered. "Then we'd better—" He stopped in midsentence. "Look, there *is* no final site-cleaning checklist. I made it up. I just wanted an excuse to tell you something." My heart was beating wildly. *Could this be the moment I'd waited for all summer?* I wondered. Peter's voice sounded hoarse as he continued. "You're really a great employee, and I wish you'd reconsider your decision to leave. I promise I won't give you any more grief for the rest of the summer."

I didn't say anything. I *couldn't* say anything. It hurt too much. I wanted to shake Peter, to make him care about me. But all he cared about was not having to replace a hardworking employee. I stood there trying to regain my composure, but it wouldn't come back. Maybe it was just that I was tired, or maybe it was because I'd truly hoped that Peter cared for me. Whatever the reason, I began to cry.

"Hey, don't do that!" Peter said. He held a handkerchief toward me. There was a new tenderness in Peter's voice. "Look, I don't blame you if you never want to speak to me again, but don't let me ruin your summer here."

"Peter," I asked, "what did I do to make you so mad at me?"

He shrugged.

"Really," I said. "I'd like to know. I know I've made some mistakes—trying to be cool and knowledgeable—but all I ever did to you was try to make you like me."

Peter sighed and turned away from me. "This is going to sound pretty dumb, I guess, but it happens to be the truth. When I first saw you get off that bus, I—well, I felt something special. And as I showed you around that first day, I began to hope that we'd spend a lot of our free time together."

Peter sighed again, but he still wouldn't look at me. "Then something happened to you. You didn't seem like the same person. Instead, you acted so phony. I hated the way you were acting, and I told myself that I didn't want anything to do with you. But then one day, I happened to see you helping the kids fish, and I was crazy about you all over again. Then you went back to being phony again. You know, from time to time I'd sneak in and watch you work with those little kids, and every time I'd think I wanted to get to know you better. I couldn't make any sense of it. Finally, I just got so frustrated that I started cutting you down every time I saw you. I guess somehow I was hoping to hurt you the way you were hurting me."

Clearing his throat, he continued, "None of it made any sense until the day you stormed into the office and told me off. Then I finally understood. I just didn't like the phony you—the real you had been special to me all along. Suddenly, I didn't feel so confused anymore . . . liking and hating the same girl. It was great to finally figure everything out, but by then you'd quit and I wasn't going to see you at all."

My mind was racing. "You know something funny?" I asked him. "I never even liked Cyndi—the girl I was trying to be—too much myself. And it was so incredibly hard to always have to think about what she'd say and do before I made a move. Sometimes I hated the way I was acting and the things I did. But once it got to be too much for me—once I realized how stupid it was to try to be someone I wasn't—I'd already blown my chance with you."

"If you didn't even like this Cyndi, why did you do it?" Peter asked. He looked genuinely perplexed.

Unable to risk looking at Peter, I said softly, "At first it was just to make friends. I'd even decided to give up the whole idea. Then you met me at the bus station. I knew right away that you were special. I wanted you to like me, but I was afraid that if you knew plain old Jill Novick, you wouldn't like her."

Peter didn't say anything for a minute. Then

I felt his strong arm go around my shoulders. "You know," he said, a slow grin spreading across his face. "The way I figure it, we've got good news and bad news."

"We do?" I asked, not caring as long as he kept his arm around me.

"The bad news is that we wasted half the summer not being together," he mused.

"And the good news?" I asked, turning to look into his magnificent blue eyes.

"We've still got the other half," he murmured. Then his lips brushed mine. The stars twinkled approvingly.